D0611343

Mending the Past

DeAnna Julie Dodson

Annie's®

AnniesFiction.com

Books in The Inn at Magnolia Harbor series

Where Hope Blooms
Safe Harbor
Binding Vows
Tender Melody
At Summer's End
Mending the Past
Kindred Blessings
Grateful Hearts
Christmas Gifts

. . . and more to come!

Mending the Past

Library of Congress-in-Publication Data
Mending the Past / by DeAnna Julie Dodson
p. cm.
I. Title
2019946134

AnniesFiction.com
(800) 282-6643
The Inn at Magnolia Harbor™
Series Creator: Shari Lohner
Editor: Lorie Jones
Cover Illustrator: Bonnie Leick

10 11 12 13 14 | Printed in China | 9 8 7 6 5 4 3 2 1

1

Grace

Grace Porter pushed the rollaway bed against the wall of the Dogwood Suite, then frowned.

She liked the rooms at the Magnolia Harbor Inn to be elegant and lovely, perfectly laid out, and the Dogwood was her finest accomplishment. It was a spacious, airy room drenched in sunlight from the French doors that led out to the veranda. The suite featured a gorgeous view of Lake Haven, a luxurious king-size four-poster bed, and a grand fireplace that would be put to good use now that the September nights were getting cool.

Shoving an extra bed in here completely spoiled the look she and her sister, Charlotte Wylde, had worked so hard to achieve ever since they had bought the inn.

"I know it's not ideal," Charlotte said, obviously reading her sister's thoughts. "But if we're going to cram fourteen guests into five rooms, we need to make some adjustments."

"You're right." Grace blew a strand of dark-brown hair out of her eyes, then put a fitted sheet on the spare bed. "I hope we haven't bitten off more than we can chew this time."

"With a bunch of older ladies sewing?" Charlotte asked, stuffing a plump pillow into a fresh pillowcase. "It sounds like a pretty quiet week, if you ask me."

Grace laughed softly as she topped the bed with a flat sheet and tucked it in. "Winnie would beg to differ."

Winnie Bennett was Grace and Charlotte's beloved aunt. She

lived nearby and often helped out at the inn. Grace didn't know what they would do without their aunt's assistance.

"Really?" Charlotte asked. "What did she say?"

"She tells me the women at quilting retreats can be kind of rambunctious. They tend to stay up all night, talking and eating more than sewing." Grace smiled. "Like a slumber party for grown-up girls."

Charlotte giggled, her brown eyes warm. "I guess Winnie should know. But these women aren't from The Busy Bees, are they?"

The Busy Bees was a sewing group that Winnie belonged to. Their aunt and her friends met every week at Spool & Thread, the local fabric shop, to quilt and socialize.

"No, but one of them used to be. Debbie Milner." Grace tossed one end of the coverlet to Charlotte, and they spread it over the bed. If the rollaway was hideously out of place here, at least they could make sure it appeared comfortable and inviting.

"I remember Winnie mentioning her before," Charlotte said. "It was nice of Debbie to think of staying with us for the retreat."

"I'm sure Winnie wasn't shy about reminding Debbie that her nieces own a bed-and-breakfast as soon as she heard her friend's quilting group was planning a retreat."

Charlotte grinned. "True."

Just then, the bell above the front door jingled.

"That will be one of them," Grace said. "Did we miss anything?"

"I think we're done," Charlotte replied. She smoothed back her blonde hair and snatched up the discarded pillowcases.

They hurried down the sweeping staircase and into the inn's magnificent foyer.

Waiting at the reception desk were two women in their fifties. They were surrounded by luggage. Each of them had a small rolling cart with a bag strapped to it. Sewing machines, of course.

Grace assumed the rest of the luggage contained not only their clothing but fabric and rulers and all the other quilting necessities. Winnie often said she worried about her quilting supplies slowly taking over her whole house, and her husband, Gus, agreed with her.

Grace smiled at the newcomers. "Welcome to the Magnolia Harbor Inn. I'm Grace Porter, and this is my sister, Charlotte Wylde. And here comes Winston. He's always happy to make new friends."

Winston, who was part shih tzu and part mystery, dashed over to the women, excited as usual to meet guests. The women fussed over the dog, and Winston reveled in the attention.

"You must be here for the quilting retreat," Grace said.

The first woman had short graying hair that had been permed, and behind her rhinestone glasses, her eyes were full of warmth and humor. "Yes, I'm Tess Harrison."

"And I'm Brenda Clifton," the other woman said as she peered around the room. "Are we the first ones here?"

She was shorter than her friend, and her bobbed blonde hair made her look a little younger, though Grace suspected there wasn't much difference in their ages. The biggest difference was their attitudes. Tess acted excited to be here, but Brenda apparently wished she were somewhere else.

Well, Grace would do her best to change Brenda's mind.

"You're first," Charlotte said as she went behind the desk. "Let's get you checked in. We have only five rooms, so we've added rollaway beds to some of the suites in order to fit everyone. Do you have any preferences for room assignments?"

"Carolyn and her daughter, Robin, will want to share a room," Brenda said.

Grace checked the list Debbie had e-mailed to her when she booked the retreat. The name *Brenda Clifton* was handwritten at the bottom of it. She was obviously a last-minute addition. "Carolyn and Robin McAllister?"

"That's right," Brenda replied.

"We can put them in the third-floor Wisteria Loft Suite," Charlotte said.

"Yes, and then Kathleen and Amanda will want to be in the same room," Tess remarked.

Grace checked the list again and found their names.

"They're twin sisters," Tess said. "And they told me that they're bringing an air mattress."

"We can put them in the Buttercup Suite," Charlotte said. "There should be plenty of space on the floor for a mattress."

"Any other requests for roommates?" Grace asked. "Would you two like to be in the same room?"

"That would be nice," Brenda said, then glanced at her companion. "If it's okay with you."

Tess grinned. "Of course it is. I invited you, didn't I?"

"Yes, but—"

"And dragged you all the way out here," Tess interrupted, patting her friend's shoulder. "We're going to have a good time, okay?"

Brenda nodded.

"Since you're here first, you might as well have your choice of rooms," Grace offered. "All the suites have private baths except for the Bluebell and Rosebud, which share a bath."

"What do you think?" Tess asked Brenda.

"Anything is fine, I guess."

"Well, I'd rather not room with Kathleen and Amanda," Tess said decidedly. "Unless you want to listen to them giggle all night."

"If you don't care to share a bathroom and you don't want to be in the Buttercup Suite, then that leaves the Dogwood," Charlotte said. "It's really our best."

"We'll take it," Tess said.

"It sounds wonderful," Brenda added.

"Isn't that just like you, Brenda Clifton?" someone sneered.

Grace turned to see a tall, spare woman with severe black eyebrows and unnaturally black hair knotted at the base of her neck. At her side was a petite woman with short brown hair and thick tortoiseshell glasses who seemed to be handling most of the baggage.

Brenda saw the black-haired woman, and her face paled.

"Why, hello, Libby," Tess said, sounding undaunted. "You're just in time to pick a room."

Libby glanced over at Brenda and sniffed. "It appears the best room is already taken."

"I think all the rooms are very nice," the other woman said. She smiled at Grace and Charlotte. "I'm Debbie Milner, and this is Libby Mayweather. I spoke to Grace Porter over the phone last week."

"I'm Grace." She shook Debbie's hand and introduced Charlotte. "We'd like to welcome you both to the Magnolia Harbor Inn. We're figuring out room arrangements, so if you have any preferences, please let us know."

"I'm sure you're surprised to see me here, Libby," Brenda said with a slight unsteadiness in her voice. "Tess told me the retreat was open to friends and family who like to quilt, so I thought it would be nice to get away for a while and relax."

Libby merely stared at her, pale eyes cold, then addressed Debbie. "Handle it any way you want."

"Why don't you go ahead and take the Dogwood Suite?" Brenda said. She glanced at Tess. "You don't mind, do you?"

Tess shook her head, not in disagreement but in resignation.

"The Rosebud Suite is our smallest," Grace said, "so I thought we'd put only two of you in there. You'd have to share the bath, but at least you wouldn't have a rollaway bed like the others."

Libby pursed her lips. "Are you saying you're planning to put an extra bed in my suite?"

"Yes," Charlotte said. "In order to fit everyone in, we have to add rollaway beds to some of the larger suites."

"It'll be fun," Debbie said cheerfully. "Just like a pajama party."

"No, not in my room," Libby stated. "Now could somebody show me where that is? I need to get settled in and take my medication." She glared at Brenda and then turned to Debbie. "I guess you can see to everything here."

"Sure," Debbie said. "I'll get it all straightened out."

Giving her sister a sidelong look, Charlotte grabbed a couple of the bags that were at Libby's feet. "If you'd like to follow me, I'll show you to your room."

After Charlotte and Libby were gone, Tess frowned at Brenda. "You didn't have to do that. You have as much right to that room as Libby does."

Brenda sighed. "It doesn't matter. I'm already antagonizing her simply by being here. I don't want to make it any worse."

"Okay," Tess said, her expression softer. "We'll be all right in, uh, which room did you say?"

"The Rosebud Suite," Grace told her. "But I'm afraid we're going to have a problem now. If Ms. Mayweather doesn't want a rollaway bed in the Dogwood Suite, someone in your group isn't going to have a place to sleep."

Debbie bit her lip. "Will a rollaway fit in Tess and Brenda's room?"

"It's a little snug, but it would work," Grace answered. "As long as you ladies don't find it too inconvenient."

"No, it'll be fine," Tess said.

"I don't mind sleeping on the extra bed. Is it all right if I come in with you?" Debbie asked Brenda and Tess.

For the first time Brenda's smile appeared genuine. "I think that would be great."

"I agree," Tess said. "But then who's going to room with Libby?"

Debbie winced slightly.

"And don't say Wanda," Tess added. "You know Wanda won't take any guff from her, and Libby's already mad."

"Maybe you'd better room with Libby," Brenda told Debbie. She sounded disappointed.

"For everybody's sake," Tess added.

Debbie's eyes widened behind her glasses. "But just the two of us in that big suite—"

"You'll be just fine," Tess interrupted. "The more I think about it, the better I think it will work."

"Ms. Mayweather and Ms. Milner in the Dogwood Suite," Grace said, making notes on the lists of names. "And Ms. Clifton and Ms. Harrison in the Rosebud Suite. Is that correct?"

Debbie nodded.

"Is there someone in particular you'd like to have in with you?" Grace asked Tess and Brenda.

"Frankie will want to stay with Wanda," Tess said. "Maybe you'd better put them in the same room with Kathleen and Amanda."

"All right," Grace said, making more notes. "So that fills up the Buttercup Suite. It leaves three in the Bluebell and one more in the Rosebud. Who would you like where?"

"Who's left?" Tess asked.

"Millie, Ginny, Ellen, and Jessica," Debbie answered.

"Why don't we put Jessica in with us?" Tess asked Brenda. "You like her."

Brenda looked relieved. "She's nice."

"Okay, Jessica is in with us," Tess said. "Are we set?"

"That should be fine," Grace said, making sure there was a designated bed for everyone on the list. She glanced up to see Charlotte descending the stairs. "And here's my sister to help you take your things up to your room."

Charlotte rejoined the women. "Have we decided?" she said, smiling at Brenda and Tess.

"They're going to be in the Rosebud," Grace told her. "And we're going to have to move the rollaway from the Dogwood in there too."

"Ladies, if you'll follow me, I'll show you to your suite." Charlotte picked up more bags.

Brenda and Tess wheeled their sewing machines behind them as they followed her.

"Sorry about that," Debbie said when only she and Grace were left at the front desk. "It's always something when you have a large group."

"I know it's difficult to please everyone, but we'll do our best to make sure everyone is comfortable." Grace smiled. "I understand you and my aunt Winnie are friends."

Debbie's face lit up. "Oh yes. We've known each other for a long time. Unfortunately, we haven't seen each other much the past few years."

"Did Winnie tell you about the inn?" Grace asked.

"Yes, and I thought it would be the perfect place for our retreat." Debbie scanned the room. "It's beautiful here. Of course, Winnie told me it was, but I don't think even she could do it justice."

"Thank you," Grace said. "We like it."

"Oh, and this is the famous hatbox." Debbie went over to the box that sat on one end of the desk. "Winnie told me about that too." She opened it up, revealing various small envelopes and folded bits of paper. "Do people really get answers to their problems here?"

"Some of them," Grace replied. "Sometimes people feel better simply writing down what's bothering them. They can be as anonymous as they like and still have the satisfaction of not holding the problem in. And you never know when someone might have words of wisdom to share in response."

"I'll have to mention it to Brenda and Libby." Debbie shook her head. "I feel terrible for them. They're cousins, and they have a history, as you can probably already tell."

Grace nodded, wondering what had happened between Brenda and Libby and how someone as seemingly meek as Brenda had had the courage to show up at an event that would throw them together for a week.

Sometimes it was hard not knowing what people were dealing with when they arrived at the inn, but of course it wouldn't be very professional of Grace to ask personal questions of the guests. All she could do was be available to listen and comfort. And pray.

"I'm glad my life doesn't have any complications like that," Debbie went on. "I like things straightforward."

"That's the easy way, isn't it?" Grace asked. "Not that it always turns out so simple."

"No, but if you keep your chin up and soldier on, you can eventually get through it." Debbie seemed thoughtful for a moment. "Tess encouraged Brenda to attend the retreat because she wants Brenda and Libby to have a chance to talk. But I hope Brenda doesn't regret coming."

"Please let Brenda and your other friends know that Charlotte and I are here to help in any way we can," Grace said.

"Thank you. Oh, and you did say we could store some soft drinks and snacks in your refrigerator, right?" Debbie's smile returned. "It wouldn't be a quilting retreat without snacks."

"That's what Winnie tells us. And, yes, you're welcome to keep your food in our refrigerator."

"And the meals are all set too?" Debbie asked.

"They are," Grace said. "As we discussed, we don't usually serve anything but breakfast and complimentary wine, cheese, and hors d'oeuvres every evening. But in this case, we'll provide sandwiches and salads for lunch and then heat up the casseroles and other prepared dishes your party is bringing for dinner."

"Yes," Debbie said. "Jessica is hauling everything in her car. And then we'll take turns helping you serve and clean up after each meal. Thanks again for accommodating us."

"It's not a problem," Grace assured her. "In fact, since Charlotte and I do almost everything around here ourselves, your assistance will be greatly appreciated."

The bell jingled, and the front door opened.

Debbie turned. "Speaking of Jessica, here she is." She hurried over to hug her friend and then greet the other women who had walked in with Jessica.

Winston bounded over to the women and received plenty of attention in return.

Grace counted a total of eight newcomers, though from the sudden commotion she would have guessed there were more like thirty.

If nothing else, this week would be lively.

2

Brenda

The Rosebud Suite didn't overlook the lake, but it offered a lovely view of the inn's garden. The heavy rains from earlier in the week had made all the plants lush and green, but Brenda was glad there was no more rain expected in the next few days. She didn't need anything else depressing to happen right now.

"Nice, isn't it?" Tess asked, studying the snug room with its high four-poster bed and dainty rosebud wallpaper. "I can't believe there's a huge chandelier in the bathroom. And I'm definitely taking a long bath in the claw-foot tub."

Brenda stood at the window and kept her gaze on the garden, wondering how long it would be before everything was dormant or dead.

"Why don't you take the right side of the dresser, and I'll take the left?" Tess suggested as she opened her suitcase. "Unless you want it, I'll take the left side of the bed too."

Still staring at the garden but not really seeing it, Brenda didn't respond.

"I don't know where we're supposed to meet," Tess went on. "Debbie said we'd have a big room for sewing and classes and everything. I should have asked her about it when we were downstairs. It would be nice to go ahead and set things up."

Brenda wished she could hide out in the room during the entire retreat. But eventually she'd have to go downstairs with everyone else. She'd promised to try.

"Is anyone in there?" Tess said.

Brenda took a slow, deep breath. "I shouldn't have come." Finally, she turned to face her friend. "You know that I want to patch things up with Libby, but . . ." She held out both hands. "I don't think I can do this."

"Of course you can," Tess said. "Okay, maybe I pushed you a little bit, but this was your idea in the first place. You're already here. It's too late to chicken out now."

"Libby's never going to forgive me." Brenda sat down on the wingback chair next to the fireplace and put her head in her hands. "And if she knows I want to reconcile with her, she's going to use it against me."

Brenda knew only too well how her cousin reacted when anyone showed even a hint of vulnerability. Besides, Libby had made it clear that she had good friends who would treat her right and she didn't need anyone else in her life.

"You can't make Libby change," Tess said. "But you can at least let her know you're willing to be friends again. Then you can leave the rest up to her."

"I'm afraid that being here is only going to make things worse," Brenda admitted.

"If your conflict with Libby has been hurting you all this time, then you need to do something about it," Tess said. "There's no use carrying around pain and regret the way you have, especially over something so stupid."

"I guess it seems that way," Brenda answered. "Okay, I know it is. It's stupid. But I had to stand up for myself sometime, didn't I? Now I'm sorry I did it. I should have let Libby have her way like I have my whole life and left it at that. At least we would have had the relationship we'd always had."

"And a pretty poor one it was, if you ask me," Tess said. "Look, there's nothing you can really do but let Libby know you care about her and want to talk again. That doesn't mean you have to let her push you around anymore. In fact, I'll bet she'd like you better if you didn't. At least she'd respect you more."

Brenda shrugged, even though she suspected that Tess was probably right.

"You don't have to make any big declarations at the moment," Tess said. "Let's go downstairs and see who's here and where we're going to meet and all that stuff. I think we're supposed to have Millie's meat loaf casserole thing for dinner tonight. You like that, don't you?"

"Yes." Brenda managed a small smile. "But I don't know if she'd be happy to hear it called a 'meat loaf casserole thing.'"

"True." Tess laughed, then pulled Brenda to her feet. "Come on. I want to check out everything. I'll bet the others have arrived by now."

Brenda's smile faded as the leaden weight in her stomach returned. "Maybe this wasn't such a good idea. Libby has a way of letting you know when she's upset with you."

"You should take a page from Wanda's book," Tess suggested. "Smile and do whatever you want."

"And you see how much Libby can't stand her," Brenda argued. She thought of eighty-two-year-old Wanda with her wispy hair dyed flaming red and a tattoo of a needle, thread, and scissors on her forearm. Wanda never went unnoticed, but she didn't seem to mind what anyone else thought of her.

"But Wanda doesn't care." Tess took Brenda's arm and tugged her toward the door. "Besides, you know Libby doesn't give Wanda any trouble."

"They don't have a good relationship either," Brenda retorted. "In fact, it seems like they don't have any relationship at all."

"Well, maybe not much of one, but they manage to get along when they have to." Tess opened the door. "Let's go. You'll never make things any better with your cousin if you don't even try."

Brenda hugged herself, remembering the cold look in Libby's eyes when they had met downstairs. "You saw Libby when we were checking in. She was telling everybody what she would and wouldn't have. It's like always. Either you do what she wants, or you don't exist."

Tess stood in the open doorway, that no-nonsense look on her face Brenda had seen more than a few times. "Do you want to straighten things out with her or not? I can't make that decision for you."

When Brenda didn't answer, Tess's expression softened. "If you attempt to reconcile and nothing changes, at least you'll know you tried."

As Brenda followed Tess out into the hall, she was certain that something would change. But she couldn't imagine that change being for the better.

Grace

"We are definitely going to have an interesting week," Grace told Charlotte once the new arrivals had been checked in and shown to their suites.

Charlotte gave her a mischievous grin. "I can see why they didn't want to put Wanda in the same room with Libby. That would have been like putting a blowtorch in a can of gasoline."

"She's definitely a firecracker." Grace laughed as she recalled meeting Wanda. She couldn't imagine the spunky older woman letting anyone intimidate her. "So, who's left?"

"Just the ladies up in Wisteria." Charlotte checked the list at the reception desk. "Carolyn McAllister and her daughter, Robin."

"Excuse me."

Grace turned to see Tess and Brenda, the guests staying in the Rosebud Suite. "How is everything in your room?" she asked them.

"Wonderful," Tess said. "I love it."

"I'm glad," Grace said. "Is there something I can do for you?"

"Brenda and I were just wondering where we were going to be sewing and that sort of thing."

"That'll be in the dining room. I'll show it to you." Grace led them to the room.

Grace had consulted Winnie on the setup for the quilting area, and the large room had been reconfigured according to her aunt's specifications. The dining table now stood closer to the fireplace, and rented worktables and folding chairs lined the other wall. On the polished marble floor was a maze of extension cords, some of which powered the small task lights that were on each table. Others were left free for sewing machines, irons, light boxes, and whatever else the quilters would need to plug in. Winnie had told Grace that few things could spoil a retreat faster than a shortage of tables and extension cords.

Grace was glad she had listened to her aunt's advice once she saw how pleased Tess and Brenda were with the arrangement.

"It's perfect," Tess said, then turned to her friend. "It's so much better than that class we went to last month."

"I agree," Brenda said. "I felt like a sardine packed in such a tiny space, and I didn't have anywhere to plug in my bobbin winder."

"In case anyone has something larger to press, we set up an ironing station over here," Grace told them, motioning to the oversize ironing board against another wall.

"This is great," Tess said. "And how can you not be creative with that gorgeous view of the lake?" She gave an appreciative nod. "I'm going to like it here."

Grace smiled. "Now let me show you the veranda where we'll be having most of the meals. If you would like to relax out back and enjoy the lake view until dinner is served, please feel free."

Tess raised her eyebrows. "Well, now I can tell you're not a quilter. We came to sew. If it's all right, I'm going to let everyone know it's time to get started."

"We're ready when you are," Grace assured her.

"Is everyone here?" Brenda asked.

"We're still waiting on the McAllisters," Grace replied.

"I hope Carolyn knows what she's doing bringing her daughter along," Tess remarked. "Robin is more than welcome to join us, but I'm not sure if this is the best place for her."

"Carolyn said she just wanted Robin to get out of the house," Brenda said. "But that doesn't always help."

"I guess we'll see," Tess said. Her expression brightened abruptly as she said to Grace, "You might want to break out some of the soft drinks and snacks."

Grace couldn't help but smile at her friendly directness. "We'll do that right away."

"I'm getting my sewing machine and things," Tess announced. "Come on if you're coming."

Brenda followed her.

When the women were gone, Grace decided she'd better see to the refreshments. She was almost to the kitchen when the bell above the front door jingled and the door opened.

Two women entered, and only one of them was pulling a sewing machine. They were certainly alike enough to be mother and daughter, slim and dressed with casual elegance. The mother was the shorter of the two by four or five inches, and her short brown hair was shot through with gray. They both had long-lashed brown eyes.

"Welcome to the Magnolia Harbor Inn," she said, walking over to them. "I'm Grace Porter, co-owner of the inn. You must be Carolyn and Robin McAllister."

"Yes, and thank you," Carolyn said.

"We've been expecting you. May I help you with your luggage?" Grace picked up two of their suitcases and escorted them to the reception desk. "You're in our Wisteria Loft Suite. It's on the third floor, and you'll have the room to yourselves."

"Wonderful," Carolyn said. "Robin isn't a quilter, so a suite out of the way of everyone else is exactly what we need."

"There's plenty to do if you don't want to sew," Grace told the younger woman. "You might enjoy spending some time at the lake. Do you swim?"

"I think I'd rather draw the lake than swim in it," Robin said, smiling slightly.

"That works. I think you'll like it out there, especially at dawn and dusk. I can't draw stick figures myself, but some mornings when I look out there, I wish I could somehow capture it on paper."

Robin's smile became a little more convincing. "It sounds beautiful. And I do like the early evening when it's quiet."

"I know exactly what you mean," Grace said. "It's as if you have the whole world to yourself. At least for a few minutes."

"Yeah," Robin said, running her fingers through her long ponytail as she pulled it over one shoulder.

"Would you like to go ahead and put your sewing machine and other supplies in the dining room?" Grace asked Carolyn. "That's where you'll all be working. I can take the rest of your things up when I show your daughter the suite."

"Thank you. That would be great." Carolyn scanned the room. "Has everyone else checked in?"

"Yes, they have. You're the last ones to arrive," Grace told her. "I showed Brenda and Tess the dining room a few minutes ago, and they went to get their things and round up everyone else."

"Are you going to be all right for a little while?" Carolyn asked her daughter. "You can always come down and sit with us. I'm sure I have plenty of fabric if you'd like to sew."

"I'll be fine in the room," Robin said. "I'll unpack and maybe take a nap. It's fine."

Carolyn gave her daughter a peck on the cheek. "If you want company, come down anytime."

Robin ducked her head. "Yeah, okay."

Grace pointed out the dining room to Carolyn, then picked up her suitcases and began to lead Robin to the stairs.

They hadn't even taken the first step before Winston raced over to them.

"Where have you been?" Grace asked him good-naturedly. "Sleeping in front of the window, I suppose. Robin, this is Winston. He loves new people, and if you need somebody to hang out with, he's a great choice."

Robin got down on one knee to pet him. "Hi," she said softly. "How are you?"

Winston gazed up at her, adoration in his eyes, and wagged his tail.

"He's a good listener too," Grace said as the three of them headed up the stairs. "He never interrupts or breaks a confidence."

Grace was almost surprised when Robin laughed. It wasn't much of a laugh, but it was something.

"I'll keep that in mind," Robin promised.

Once Grace had left Robin and her luggage up in the loft with Winston to keep her company, she went back down to the dining room.

Carolyn was setting up her sewing machine. None of the other quilters had come down yet.

"Whenever you're ready to go upstairs, your suite is on the third floor," Grace said. "You can't miss it."

"Thank you for taking Robin to our room. I promised her that if she would come with me to this retreat, I would give her all the alone time she wanted." There was something wistful in Carolyn's expression. "I'm trying not to hover."

Whatever was going on with her and her daughter, Grace couldn't help but sympathize. Her own son, Jake, was grown and on his own, but that didn't mean she didn't want to take on the world on his behalf anytime he had troubles. "She didn't want to come?"

Carolyn winced. "Is it that obvious?"

"It's sort of hard to miss." Grace pulled out the chair next to Carolyn and sat down. "Is there anything we can do for Robin while she's here? Anything she wants to do? A favorite dessert? I know your group has all the meals planned out, but my sister is a gourmet chef. She could probably whip up anything your daughter would like."

"Thank you for that, but I've tried everything I know for the past eight months. None of it has helped. And, yes, I know people have to grieve in whatever way and for whatever period they need to. I understand that. But I want so much for her to start living again."

There was such anguish in the woman's eyes that a lump formed in Grace's throat. "Did she lose someone?" She stopped herself. "I'm sorry. I don't mean to pry."

"Robin's fiancé passed away."

Grace didn't know what to say. There was nothing she could say. It was a tragedy. "I'm very sorry. Your daughter must have been devastated."

"It wasn't so bad at first," Carolyn said. "I mean, of course she was heartbroken, but she handled it. She said she knew her life had to go on. But later, when she had to cancel their wedding plans and return gifts and send out notices that the wedding would not take place, it really hit her. He was never coming back. She wasn't going to be married. She was alone."

"I lost my husband in a train accident a long time ago," Grace told her. "I didn't even think it was real at first. Part of me thought he'd eventually come home and things would be like they always had been. I guess it's the shock of it, and then you realize you have to keep doing all the normal things you've always done, but now you have to do them by yourself. At least I had our son to think of. He was my reason for going on."

"I'm sorry for your loss." Carolyn blotted her eyes with her fingertips, then started fiddling with her rotary cutter and ruler. "The worst part right now is that they were supposed to be married this afternoon at five."

Grace put a hand over her heart. "Oh, poor Robin."

"I told her I wouldn't come to the retreat this year if she'd rather I stayed home with her, but she said that would be worse than having to come with me." Carolyn shook her head. "Robin says she's fine. I think she's all right most days, but she doesn't want to do much of anything. She goes to work. She comes home. She draws. She reads. That's all."

Grace nodded. "Creative arts can be therapeutic."

"All my friends tell their husbands that quilting is cheaper than therapy," Carolyn said.

They both smiled.

"Does Robin live with you?" Grace asked.

"She does now. She had her own apartment before the accident, and Jason was going to move in there after the wedding. Once he was gone, she couldn't stand to be there anymore. I'm a widow and live alone, so I convinced her to move in with me. She promised it would be a temporary arrangement. But that was months ago, and she hasn't even started searching for another place. Not that I mind. I'd love for her to stay forever, but I know it's not good for her. She was always so independent before."

"Give her time," Grace said gently. "It may not seem like much, but she's taken a huge step in coming here with you, especially today of all days."

"To be honest, I was a little surprised that she decided to join me. That's why I'm trying not to hover. It's a start, isn't it?" Carolyn asked, a pleading look in her eyes.

"It's a great start," Grace assured her. "And if anybody can make her feel better, it's my dog, Winston. He met us on the stairs a little bit ago, and I left him and Robin together in your suite. He has a way of comforting people who are hurting."

"Robin loves dogs," Carolyn said. "It'll be nice for her to spend time with him. She hasn't had a pet since she went to college."

"There's a hatbox on the desk in our reception area where people often leave notes about whatever they're struggling with," Grace said. "Robin is welcome to use it if she'd like to. Once in a while, people get helpful answers or simply a word of encouragement. It can be anonymous or not, whatever the writer is comfortable with."

"Thank you. I'll make sure and let her know." She glanced toward the dining room's open door at the sound of approaching voices. "I guess it's time to start sewing. Thanks for listening."

"Anytime," Grace said. "A lot of people tell me they like the peacefulness of our inn. I hope you and your daughter will too."

The room was already filling with the chattering voices of the other twelve women.

Carolyn gave her a wry look. "I don't know how much peace anyone gets during a quilting retreat."

4

Debbie

Apart from the hum of a couple of sewing machines, the dining room was relatively silent the next morning. Her mother would have called it a Sunday quiet.

Most everyone had stayed up until the small hours of the morning, but one by one they had reached a stopping point, set aside their projects for the night, and gone to bed.

Debbie didn't know if any of them had come downstairs for the breakfast provided by the inn. She wasn't much of a breakfast eater herself, so she didn't mind waiting until lunch was served.

Across the table from her, Amanda and Kathleen were working on some paper-pieced blocks and discussing the latest TV series they were binge-watching. They were both tall and thin and had identical platinum haircuts. Amanda was in pink, and Kathleen was in blue. That was the only way Debbie was ever able to tell the twins apart.

Millie, Frankie, Ellen, and Ginny were cutting out pieces for the guild's raffle quilt at the next table, and Jessica was at the ironing board pressing them.

Everyone else had just gotten back from the local church. Everyone but Libby, who had told Debbie that she would join the group when she was ready.

"Anybody home?"

"Winnie!" Debbie stood up from her sewing machine and practically flew across the dining room to the woman who had walked in. Somehow, despite being Debbie's senior by more than ten years,

Winnie appeared as bright-eyed and lively as ever. Just as pretty and put together too. "How did I end up getting older and you still look the same?"

Winnie gave Debbie a big hug. "Nonsense. I feel every bit my age when I get out of bed in the morning."

"It's so good to see you again," Debbie said. "Grace and Charlotte didn't mention when you'd be able to come by. How are you?"

"Doing well," Winnie said. "How about you?"

"I'm fine," Debbie said, then changed the subject. "Now let me introduce you to some of our group. Ladies, this is Winnie Bennett. Her nieces own the inn, and some of the women from her bee will be coming by to teach us some new quilting and piecing techniques."

Frankie clasped her hands together. "I heard we're supposed to learn a new appliqué method. The sample Debbie showed us was beautiful, and I can't wait to hear about it."

"I'll be teaching that on Tuesday," Winnie replied, glancing over at Debbie for confirmation.

Debbie nodded. "We'll have a class on transferring photos to fabric tomorrow, appliqué on Tuesday, crazy quilting and embellishments on Wednesday, strip piecing on Thursday, and stitch and flip on Friday. So, besides the projects we brought with us, we'll have plenty to do."

There was a general murmur of agreement.

"I'll let you ladies return to your sewing," Winnie said. "I just came by to check with Debbie about our schedule and the supplies we'll need."

Debbie rummaged in her bag and pulled out the schedule she had created for the classes. "Let's make sure we're on the same page about everything. Is there someplace we can talk?"

"The back veranda would be nice," Winnie suggested. "And I'll bet I can find us both a cup of coffee somewhere too."

Charlotte was more than accommodating, and soon Debbie and Winnie were settled on the veranda, enjoying the lake view and drinking cups of rich, aromatic coffee.

Debbie noticed Robin sitting under a tree with a sketch pad in her lap, but she didn't seem to be drawing anything. Farther on, two children were playing with their dad at the edge of the water. Beyond them, some boys were trying to fish, but they were making too much commotion to actually catch anything.

Winnie smiled as she surveyed the lake. "Gorgeous, isn't it? I'm glad you and your friends are staying here."

"It's beautiful," Debbie agreed. "And you live nearby?"

"Right down the road," Winnie said. "It gives me a chance to drop by and visit with my nieces as often as I can. When I'm not at home with my husband and my cat."

"How are Gus and Phoebe?" Debbie asked. "Phoebe was such a cute little thing the last time I saw her."

"Gus is doing well. Phoebe's about the same. Spoiled rotten, of course." Winnie took a sip of coffee. "What about you? How's your back? I heard you had to have surgery."

"Oh, it was nothing," Debbie said. "It was over and done with last year, but thanks for asking. Besides, I can't complain, and even if I did, nobody would want to hear." She chuckled.

Winnie studied her. "You seem tired."

Debbie kept her expression bland. Was it obvious? "It's not easy putting together one of these retreats. But you know how it is. You've been there yourself."

"I have, but I also don't have the least bit of trouble with boundaries," Winnie said. "Are you sure you didn't get roped into this? I'm afraid you're too nice sometimes."

"Somebody had to be in charge, and it wasn't that hard. Your nieces were great about the rooms and the meals and everything." Debbie thought for a moment. "But I am a little worried about Libby Mayweather. Do you know her?"

There was a sudden touch of amusement in Winnie's hazel eyes. "Oh yes, but I haven't seen her in years. Not since she stopped coming to the Raleigh retreat. What's going on with her?"

"Her knee's pretty bad, but she refuses to do anything about it," Debbie replied. "I think she needs a total replacement, but she won't even talk to her doctor about it. When she can't stand the pain, she takes some pills."

"That's terrible," Winnie said.

"To be honest, I don't know how Libby manages to get around. Wanda says it's because she's so stubborn."

Winnie laughed. "That sounds like Wanda all right. Is she here?"

"Yes, and I'm sure she'd love to see you," Debbie said. "Why don't you stay for lunch? You could say hello to Wanda and meet the rest of the ladies. There's always plenty of food."

"I'd love to," Winnie said, smiling. "There's a casserole in the oven, so Gus will be fine on his own."

"That's wonderful," Debbie said. "You'll like the group."

"I'm sure I will," Winnie answered. "What were you saying about Libby?"

Debbie sipped her coffee as she considered how much she should tell Winnie. "We're rooming together in the big suite that overlooks the lake. The Dogwood Suite."

"It has a lovely view," Winnie said.

"Yes, it does," Debbie said. "But I'm not sure if Libby is enjoying it, even though she's been up there all morning. She didn't go to church or join the rest of us to sew."

"Is her knee bothering her that much?" Winnie asked. "Maybe you should persuade her to see a doctor."

"I don't think it's that," Debbie admitted. "Her cousin Brenda showed up at the retreat, and Libby wasn't expecting her."

"Why is Libby upset about seeing her cousin?"

"She and Brenda haven't gotten along for a few years now. Tess Harrison invited Brenda, and they asked me not to let Libby know. Now I'm wondering if Libby's mad at me because I didn't tell her ahead of time."

Winnie winced. "It's probably not a great idea to surprise someone like that, especially when it concerns a family feud."

"I know, but Brenda really wants to work things out with her, and Libby won't even talk to her on the phone. Brenda thought this might be a good opportunity to at least get to be on speaking terms. I hated to tell her no, but I'm questioning if it was the right thing to do."

"It can't be undone at this point. Maybe it'll end up being a good thing after all. What did Libby say?"

Debbie sighed. "Not much of anything. I didn't bring it up when we were in our room last night, and she didn't say anything to me this morning except that she'd come downstairs when she was ready. I haven't had a chance to talk to Brenda either. But I was thinking I'd tell both of them about the hatbox in the foyer."

Winnie's eyes warmed. "It wouldn't hurt."

Debbie considered for a long moment, feeling an ache in her heart that she couldn't show on her face. "Do you ever read them?" she asked finally. "The notes people put in there."

"Sometimes. When I feel led."

"Do you ever answer them?" Debbie bit her lip as soon as she said it. Was she giving too much away? Maybe not. Winnie didn't look as if she thought the question was more than idle curiosity.

"Sometimes," Winnie repeated. "When I feel led."

Debbie gazed at the lake again. The boys trying to fish were gone. Robin was concentrating on whatever she was drawing. The children and their father were swimming. Robin hadn't seemed to have noticed them.

"Well, Libby probably won't want to, but maybe Brenda would feel better if she wrote down how she was feeling right now," Debbie said. "I'll make sure Brenda knows about the box."

"She's more than welcome." Winnie drained her coffee. "I'd better call Gus and let him know I'll be staying for lunch. I'm looking forward to meeting the rest of your friends." She got up and walked away.

Debbie watched her go. She sat for several minutes listening to the distant laughter of the man and his children as they played in the water. Then she reached into her bag and pulled out a notebook and a pen.

I don't know what to do, she wrote, the letters small and uncertain. *I don't know how to even begin getting out of this mess I've made, and I'm so afraid someone is going to find out . . .*

5

Grace

"Sorry I'm late," Grace said as she came into the kitchen.

Charlotte glanced up from the pot she was stirring on the stove, and Winnie turned in her seat at the island.

"No problem," Charlotte said. "I was just heating up the vegetable soup I made yesterday."

"Wonderful. Nothing tastes as good as soup in September when the weather finally starts to cool down." Grace set down her purse and the large paper bag she had brought in with her, then hugged Winnie. "I hope you're staying for lunch."

Her aunt nodded. "I'm looking forward to meeting the quilting group."

"Is there something I can help you with?" Grace asked Charlotte.

"I have everything for the sandwiches over there if you want to start putting them together." Charlotte motioned to the counter, where bread and cold cuts were laid out with assorted vegetables.

"Sure." Grace washed her hands, then went over to the counter. "It would be easier for us if we set everything out for the ladies to make their own sandwiches. Then we wouldn't have to ask them what they want. What do you think?"

"I think less work for us is great," Charlotte said with a grin. "Should we put the soup in a tureen and let them help themselves?"

"I don't see why not," Winnie said. "During most retreats, the women bring the food and fix it and clean up afterward. I'm sure they won't mind."

"They'll be helping us tidy up too," Grace added.

"Sounds good." Charlotte stirred the pot one more time and then leaned down to get the soup tureen out of the lower cabinet. "So, where were you? Was church late?"

The sisters took turns attending church so one of them could remain at the inn when they had guests.

"I stopped by Spencer's on the way home," Grace replied.

Spencer Lewis was their neighbor who lived at Blossom Hill Farm, where he grew pecans. He was a retired intelligence analyst for the FBI, and he was always willing to lend a hand at the inn whenever Grace and Charlotte needed him.

"And?" Charlotte asked.

Instead of answering, Grace shook the paper bag she had brought in with her.

Charlotte whirled around at the heavy rattling sound. "Oh, is it time? Is it finally time?"

"Spencer said these are the first ones." Grace opened the bag to let her sister see the fresh pecans inside. "He's so proud of this crop."

"What are we waiting for? Let's try them." Charlotte took two pecans and cracked the shells with the handle of one of the kitchen knives in the block on the counter.

They all sampled the nuts.

"They're delicious," Grace said.

"So fresh and tasty," Winnie remarked.

Charlotte cracked a few more pecans. "I'm going to experiment with these and see if I can add some recipes featuring pecans to my new cookbook."

"Good idea," Grace said. "By the way, how's it coming?"

"It's all right. You know how it is. Every time I write a new one, I wonder why I ever thought I could write a book in the first place. Then

I absolutely know I'll never be able to finish, and if I do finish, I'm sure it'll be the worst book ever and my publisher will fire me on the spot."

Grace laughed. "And when you get the book back from the printer, you always love it."

Charlotte laughed too. "Of course."

"The title is perfect," Winnie said. "*Comfort and Cheer from Magnolia Harbor Inn*."

"It makes you feel cozy," Grace said.

"Now that I'm thinking about pecans, I wonder if I could use the recipe for chicken stuffed with pecans, broccoli, and cream cheese that Dean and I came up with a couple of months ago." Charlotte grinned, her dark-brown eyes dancing. "I'd give him partial credit for it."

Dean Bradley was the owner of The Tidewater, the small contemporary inn and restaurant on the other side of the lake. Charlotte and Dean had a friendly rivalry about their cooking, and they didn't often collaborate.

"I thought he was trying to get his own cookbooks published," Grace said.

"True, but he'd have to give me credit for that one if he used it." Charlotte ate another pecan. "But as long as I have these pecans, I guess I can come up with something totally original."

"And if you eat them all, you'll have to find something else to base your recipe on," Grace teased as she closed the bag and put it away.

"Spoilsport," Charlotte said with a grin.

Grace turned back to the sandwich fixings and began transferring them onto serving platters. "I told Spencer about the quilters' retreat, and he showed me some of the quilts his great-grandmother made in the 1930s. I had no idea he had anything like that."

"Really? Do you think he'd bring them over?" Winnie asked. "I'm sure the ladies would love to see them."

"That's a great idea," Grace said. "The quilts are fascinating and in amazing shape for how old they are."

"Then the ladies will be thrilled to take a peek at them," Winnie said.

"But do you think the group will have any time to spare?" Grace asked. "They already have a lot of activities planned."

"Maybe you should check with someone in the group about it," Winnie suggested.

"I'll do that," Grace said, adding a few more pieces of cheese to the platter she was arranging.

"Do you think Spencer would mind?" Charlotte asked.

"I don't think so," Grace replied. "He was happy to show them to me, but I doubt if he'd want to be the one to present them to the women."

"I'd be glad to show them to the group and talk about them," Winnie said.

"Terrific." Grace smiled at her aunt. "Thank you."

"My pleasure." Winnie paused. "Speaking of the guests, I was talking to Debbie earlier, and I'm a bit concerned about her."

"Why?" Charlotte asked. "What's wrong?"

"I'm not sure," Winnie said. "But she seems very tired."

"Perhaps it's because of the retreat," Grace said. "It sounds like she spent a lot of time organizing it, and now she's busy keeping it on track."

"Yes, that's what Debbie said when I asked her," Winnie answered. "But I'm afraid something else is bothering her."

Their conversation was interrupted by a knock at the back door. A moment later, Dean popped into the kitchen, a cheeky grin on his handsome face. He held out a plate covered in plastic wrap. "I come bearing gifts."

Charlotte immediately took the plate from him. "What's this?"

"Apricot bars with a graham cracker crust and slivered almonds on top," Dean answered. "And my own secret ingredient. Want to give me your opinion?"

Charlotte and Grace helped themselves to a piece.

"I'd love to try it, but I need to watch my sugar," Winnie said. She had diabetes, and she kept it under control with diet and exercise.

Grace closed her eyes. "Oh, good heavens, that's wonderful. It melts in your mouth."

His brown eyes sparkled.

"Don't make him any smugger than he already is," Charlotte said, grinning at him.

"What do you think?" Dean asked. "Will they do?"

Charlotte made a show of acting uncertain, and then she nodded. "Absolutely delicious. What's the secret ingredient?"

"It will remain a secret," he said, his eyes twinkling again. "But I'll leave you the plate if you want."

Grace grabbed it. "We want it."

"What's the catch?" Charlotte asked. "You didn't come over here just to bring us a treat, did you?"

Dean shrugged. "Why not? Your opinion means a lot to me." He paused. "And I wanted to ask you a favor."

"I thought so," Charlotte said.

"It will be a breeze for you, and I would be very grateful."

Charlotte didn't say anything as she regarded him suspiciously.

"It would put me in your debt the next time you need a favor," Dean added.

"You'd better take him up on it," Grace said to her sister.

"What is it?" Charlotte asked.

"Something you're a whiz at." Dean turned his most charming smile on her. "With all your experience and success, it won't be the least bit of trouble to do."

"Laying it on a little thick, aren't you?" Charlotte said, crossing her arms over her chest.

"It's only the truth," he said with perfect innocence. "What do you say?"

"Well, I'm certainly not going to promise to do something before I know what it is," Charlotte responded.

"You know I've been wanting to publish my own cookbook, right?" Dean asked.

Charlotte nodded.

"I've been studying the guidelines from several cookbook publishers," he said. "Based on those, I've written a couple of sample recipes and an introduction. I was wondering if you might check them over for me and tell me what they need. Please?"

Grace knew how hard her sister worked on her cookbooks. Charlotte told her the most effortless-looking prose was a product of the hardest work. How would Charlotte have the time and energy to work on someone else's book in addition to her own?

"It takes just about every minute I have to run this place and write books too," Charlotte hedged.

"I know, especially since that's exactly what I've been trying to do over at my place," Dean said. "I realize I'm asking a huge favor, and I promise I'm not going to expect you to do anything but read my intro and two recipes. Just to see if I'm getting the hang of it. Would you? I'll pay you for your time."

"Dean."

"I don't want to ruin my chance with these publishers," he continued. "If I send something off before it's ready, I doubt they'll review my work a second time."

"Dean," Charlotte repeated.

"Will you at least consider it?" he asked.

"No."

Dean winced and then nodded, obviously resigned.

Charlotte smiled. "No, because I've already considered it. And I'd be happy to help you."

"That's wonderful." Dean beamed at Charlotte as if he had just won the lottery. "Thank you so much. I promise I won't bug you about this ever again."

"It's not a big deal," Charlotte said. "I can only give you my opinion. Every publisher is different, so what one likes, another might not. And I don't mind at all. I would have loved it if someone who already knew the ropes had helped me when I was first trying to get published."

"They always say you get only one chance to make a first impression," Dean commented. "I don't want to blow mine."

"I can't imagine you would, but we'll do our best to make sure you don't."

"Can I e-mail you my ideas?" he asked.

"Sounds good," Charlotte said.

"I'll send them to you soon," Dean told Charlotte, then addressed Grace and Winnie. "You two have got a great sister and niece."

"I agree," Grace said, smiling.

Winnie smiled too. "You don't have to remind me."

"Thanks again for checking out my ideas," Dean said to Charlotte. "I seriously appreciate it. If you ever need something, call me first. Deal?"

"Deal," Charlotte said.

"Enjoy the apricot bars." With a wave and a promise to see them soon, Dean was gone.

"Are you okay with helping him out?" Grace asked.

"I'm happy to do it," Charlotte answered.

"I'm proud of you, and your mother would be too," Winnie said, referring to Hazel Wylde, Grace and Charlotte's mother and Winnie's older sister who had passed away years ago.

"Thanks. But I know he has some great ideas." Charlotte shrugged. "Besides, we're focused on different kinds of recipes. He wants to do a cookbook specifically for men."

Grace gave her a quick hug. "Dean was right about one thing. I do have a great sister."

"And I have a great niece," Winnie chimed in as she patted Charlotte's shoulder.

"Oh, stop," Charlotte said, laughing.

Grace went back to her platter of sandwich makings. "So how were things here this morning? Anything I should know about?"

"It was pretty quiet actually," Charlotte said. "Most of the ladies have been in the dining room quilting. I think Libby is still in her room unless she came down after I started lunch. Robin has been out by the lake since about ten."

"I'll go outside and let her know lunch is ready," Grace said. "I want her to feel welcome."

"Do you think Robin will eat with everyone else?" Charlotte asked. "She doesn't seem to want much company besides Winston."

"All I can do is let her know," Grace said. She stood very still for a moment, listening. "The quilters seem pretty quiet right now." She smiled. "At least I can't hear them, which is an improvement from last night."

"Don't count on it lasting very long," Winnie remarked with a laugh. "It can get awfully loud when women gather to quilt."

As if on cue, there was a burst of laughter from the other side of the kitchen door and then a knock. It was the twins, Amanda and Kathleen.

"We've come to see if we can help you with lunch," Amanda said.

"Thank you. We appreciate it." Grace handed her a stack of plates and gave Kathleen the corresponding number of knives, spoons, and forks. "Please set everything out on the veranda."

"No problem," Kathleen said.

"If you'd like to let everyone know that lunch is ready," Grace said, "we'll be out with the food in a few minutes."

"We'll tell them," Amanda said. "Come on."

Amanda and her sister hurried out with the plates and silverware.

Grace finished with the serving platters and picked one up. "Ready?"

Charlotte poured the soup into the tureen, then grabbed a ladle. "Let's go."

"We don't want to disappoint a bunch of hungry quilters," Winnie said as she took the other serving platter.

Grace opened the door and held it for Winnie and Charlotte. They walked onto the veranda and arranged the food table.

"I'm going to see if Robin would like to eat with everybody," Grace told Charlotte and Winnie. "I'll be right back."

She walked down to the lake. Robin was sitting on the ground with her sketch pad in her lap, though she wasn't actually drawing. She seemed to be gazing at the water. Or maybe she wasn't seeing it at all.

"Hi," Grace said when she got closer, not wanting to startle her.

Robin glanced up, her face pale under the smattering of freckles on her nose, her long hair whipped by the wind. "Oh. Hi."

"It's beautiful outside, isn't it?" Grace asked.

Robin nodded as she closed her sketch pad.

Grace couldn't help but catch a glimpse of the drawing. There wasn't much to it yet, just a few bold lines, some darks and lights, but it was clearly the drawing of an attractive young man. It was hard to say what his expression was. He wasn't smiling, but he didn't appear sad or angry. Hopeful, maybe. Ready to meet life head-on. Was that how Robin remembered the love she had lost?

"You're very talented," Grace remarked when Robin didn't say anything. "I wish I could draw something that actually looked like what it's supposed to be."

"It's not that hard," Robin said finally. "People sometimes think it's all about drawing lines, but most of it is figuring out what is light and what is dark. And like most things, it's about studying and practicing. I enjoy it."

"It's nice to do something creative. Something that expresses what you're thinking."

Robin shrugged. "Sometimes I draw things the way I wish they were."

"There's nothing wrong with that," Grace said. "I know a writer who says she writes because she wants to create a world that's better than what we have."

Robin gave her a brittle little smile. "I wish it was that easy."

Grace didn't say anything. If Robin wanted to talk, she didn't want to scare her away.

"How do you start again?" Robin asked at last, gazing at the lake. "I mean, when you think everything is going exactly the way you want it to, and then all of a sudden it isn't?" She turned to Grace. "Mom told me your husband suddenly died many years ago."

Grace nodded.

"Do you think of him often?"

"Not as much anymore," Grace admitted, and she sat on the ground next to Robin. "Some of our son's mannerisms remind me of him. I remember his birthday and our anniversary. When somebody gets married, I remember our wedding. I think of him on our son's birthday. Those things used to be painful for me, but now they make me smile. I loved him very much, and I would have rather had the time with him that I did than to have been spared the pain of losing him."

Robin was silent for a moment. "So, you stopped caring that he was gone?"

"No, but it's human nature to heal," Grace replied. "It's like having a wound that causes a lot of damage. It doesn't bleed forever. The body heals and then you have a scar, but the scar doesn't hurt like the wound once did."

"I want to heal," Robin said, tears springing to her eyes. "Sometimes I feel like I am, and then I feel bad, like I didn't love him enough. I'm afraid that if I try to enjoy life again, something else will happen to ruin it all. My mom wants me to get back to the way I was, but I don't know if I ever can."

"You probably won't," Grace said. "I'm not the same person I was before my husband died. But I'm also not the same person I was before I got married or before I had a child. Life changes us, and there's no going back."

"It's what's ahead that scares me," Robin murmured, staring at the ground. "And then I feel stupid for being scared. After all, I'm not the only one who's ever lost somebody."

"That doesn't make it any less painful. All you can do is keep going." Grace patted her hand. "At whatever speed feels right to you."

Robin nodded, but she didn't say anything more.

Grace stood up and gave the young woman a hopeful smile. "I came out to see if you wanted to have lunch with everybody else. My sister made a delicious vegetable soup, and there's a variety of sandwich fixings."

"Thanks," Robin said, "but I'm not ready to come in yet. I'll get something to eat later."

"Anytime," Grace said. "Just let me know. I'll be happy to do whatever I can to help." She stood there for another moment, but Robin seemed lost in her thoughts. Clearly the conversation was over.

When Grace got to the veranda, she glanced back one last time. Robin had opened her sketch pad and was drawing again.

6

Brenda

On Saturday afternoon and all day Sunday, the quilters had spent their time however they liked, finishing their own projects or working on the guild raffle quilt or even piecing one of the many charity quilts the guild provided.

Now it was Monday morning. After warming up with some free sewing in the dining room, it was time for the first of the classes to be taught by members of The Busy Bees quilting group.

Brenda hadn't made much of an attempt to talk to Libby so far. She had tried a few times during meals to say something pleasant that would invite a response. Libby always responded politely and indifferently, then immediately turned away from Brenda to talk to someone else. It was more than a little awkward.

Things would have been even worse if Tess wasn't around. Brenda didn't know what she would have done without her friend. Tess had a way of smoothing things over by filling in the uncomfortable gaps in the conversation and saying something cheerful to dispel the tension that hung between the two cousins. She was a lifesaver.

Brenda prayed Tess would be especially blessed for what she was doing, even though her efforts probably wouldn't make much difference in the long run. Libby certainly showed no sign of softening. Even now, Libby was sitting at the back of the room by herself, silently working on her intricate double-wedding-ring pattern.

The whole situation with Libby was so discouraging that Brenda considered leaving a note in the hatbox at the reception desk. Debbie had told her about the box and mentioned that the note could be anonymous. Brenda thought it might help to write her feelings down, but somehow she couldn't make herself pick up a pen.

"Okay, everybody," Debbie called out.

The sounds of sewing machines and chatter quieted.

Brenda glanced up and saw a redhead with a fair complexion standing next to Debbie at the front of the room.

"Please welcome Patty Duncan from The Busy Bees," Debbie told the group. "She's going to teach us some techniques for transferring photos to fabric."

"Let's go ahead and get started," Patty said, smiling. "Did any of you bring pictures you'd like to work with today? I've always found it's more fun to learn if you use something you're interested in."

Brenda glanced around the room at her fellow quilters. Millie brought out a few pictures of her orange tabby cat, Petey. Jessica had a lovely picture of her grandparents' wedding right after World War II. Frankie and several others had photos of their grandchildren. Wanda set out a variety of iconic shots of classic rock bands.

"Interesting," Patty said, perusing Wanda's photo collection. "Are you making something for your grandkids?"

"Are you kidding?" Wanda said, a touch of humor in her bright-blue eyes. "They don't know who any of these guys are. This quilt is for me."

"Nice," Patty told her. "And that's the beauty of making quilts based on your favorite photos. They'll always be the pictures you want to remember."

Brenda put her hand over the photo album she had packed for the retreat. It contained a variety of photos of her family, including Libby. Now she regretted her decision. Brenda should have picked something else to use in class, such as a picture of her mother or a photo of one of the cathedrals she'd visited in Europe.

"You brought a whole album," Patty said, smiling down on Brenda. "What have you got?"

Brenda forced herself not to glance at Libby. "Just some family photos from when I was growing up."

"Wonderful," Patty said. "Let's take a peek."

Brenda reluctantly opened the album.

"Oh, look at you," Ellen said, pointing at a picture of two young girls a few years apart standing next to an enormous oak tree. They were both tan from the summer sun and grinning. "And who's this?"

"That's Libby," Brenda murmured. She had wanted to bring these photos in particular, hoping they would remind her cousin of how things had once been between them, but now it seemed like an awful idea.

"Hey, Libby!" Ginny turned around and grinned. "You should check out some of these pictures."

Brenda faced Libby, her smile hopeful. "I thought you might want to see the album while we're here."

Libby stood up from her table, a slight, indulgent smile on her thin lips, and hobbled over to where Brenda was sitting. She glanced at the picture of the two girls, then flipped a few pages and studied photos of the girls accompanied by their grandmother wearing a floral housedress. Some pictures showed only their grandmother as she cooked or worked in her abundant flower garden or stood before her clapboard house dressed for church.

"Grandma loved her irises, didn't she?" Brenda ventured.

Libby turned another page, stopping at a photograph of their grandmother seated behind her old-fashioned sewing machine. "She loved sewing too. Good thing she didn't know what went on after she passed away. She might have rethought her will."

Brenda pressed her lips together. She wasn't going to react to that. Not today. Grandma had done what she had wanted to do, and Brenda didn't have to be ashamed of abiding by her wishes. She drew a deep breath and smiled again. "I'm sure everyone wants to get started on their projects. If you want to, we can look at the pictures after class. I found some good ones. Remember that puppy you had when we were—"

"What pictures are you planning to use?" Libby interrupted.

Brenda blinked at her. "I haven't decided yet. Probably some photos from when we were girls. I thought it would make a nice quilt. Maybe we could both make one."

Libby didn't respond to her cousin. Instead, she asked Patty, "What kind of permission do you need to use pictures in your quilts?"

Patty frowned. "No one has ever asked me that before. I'll have to check into it. As far as I know, you can always use your own photos. I suppose you can use any images you find if you're not going to sell them in any way, but I'm not positive. Is there a picture you want to use that you're not sure about?"

Libby focused on the album once more. This time, she studied a photo of the two girls holding hands and grinning in identical dresses. Grandma had made the dresses as a surprise that summer. "I just wanted to know if someone can use a picture of you without your permission." She smirked at Brenda. "I'd hate to have to sue somebody."

The room was silent as Libby hobbled back to her table and sat down.

Patty glanced at Debbie, obviously wondering if she should go on with the class.

Debbie smiled. "Brenda, why don't you pick something with only your grandmother in it for now? And, Libby, I didn't see what you were going to do."

"Well, come look if you want to," Libby huffed.

Debbie went over to Libby, and the two talked quietly.

"You have a lot of nice pictures in there," Tess told Brenda. "And we're only learning, so there's no need to use all your best ones right away." She pointed to a photo. "I like this calico cat. She's pretty."

"Thanks," Brenda said. "I had Rosebud when I was little."

"Oh, what a darling," Millie said, peering over Brenda's shoulder. "Did I show you this one of Petey?" She held out a picture of her tabby cat.

The other ladies chimed in, and soon the awkwardness had passed. At least Brenda managed to pretend like it had.

The class turned out to be enjoyable and informative, and even Libby seemed to have a good time. She deigned to speak to Brenda once or twice, the barbs in her words apparently going unnoticed by everyone else in the group. Tess stayed close to Brenda, still smoothing over any uncomfortable moments, making them at least bearable until the class was over and the group broke for lunch.

"I like it," Tess remarked, surveying Brenda's project.

"Thanks," Brenda said. She'd put the picture of her cat Rosebud into a small quilted block that she'd made into a mug rug.

"Are you coming?" Tess asked when Brenda didn't get up.

"I'll be there in a minute," Brenda said as she gathered her things. She'd be coming back here after they ate, but she hated leaving a mess behind. She preferred having everything set right, even if it created more work. "You go ahead before the twins take all the deviled eggs."

"Okay, I'd better hurry," Tess said, laughing.

A moment later, Brenda was alone in the dining room. She picked up her photo album, meaning to put it away with her other things, but then she opened it again.

She began at the front of the album, studying the two girls who had been best friends. Libby holding Brenda as a baby with Grandma keeping a watchful eye. Libby blowing out six candles on her birthday cake and three-year-old Brenda clapping plump little hands in excitement. She and Libby riding bicycles, her own with training wheels and Libby's older, a little battered, too big for even her lanky frame. Both of them wearing the dresses Grandma had made . . .

"I'm sorry."

Brenda startled at the voice and turned to see Grace in the doorway with a trash bag. "Oh." Brenda blotted her eyes with one hand, then shut the album and slid it into her bag. "Come on in. We're done till after lunch."

Grace regarded her for a moment, then started collecting loose bits of trash she found on the tables and in the large pencil holders that were used for threads and other sewing trash. "I'm glad I caught you. I talked to my aunt about something, and she said I'd better check with someone in the group."

Brenda was a little puzzled. "I'm only a guest at this retreat, but I'll be glad to help if I can."

"Well, our neighbor Spencer has a pecan farm—"

"We'd love to have pecans," Brenda said immediately.

"Charlotte's already working on some pecan-friendly recipes," Grace said. "I'm sure there will be enough pecans for the whole group to have a taste if they'd like. But I wanted to ask you about something else."

"What is it?"

"I didn't know this until recently, but Spencer has a few quilts his great-grandmother made in the 1930s. They're in amazing shape for how old they are, and Winnie suggested that your group might like to see them. What do you think?"

"Every quilter I've ever met enjoys seeing other people's quilts, especially the antique ones," Brenda answered. "I'm sure the group would love to have Spencer show them to us and talk about them."

Grace laughed softly. "I don't know about him presenting them.

That's probably a little out of his comfort zone, especially when the subject is quilts. But Winnie said she'd be happy to get information about the quilts and share it with the group."

"That sounds wonderful," Brenda said. "Oh, Winnie's supposed to teach an appliqué class. Maybe she could bring along Spencer and his quilts then."

"Great idea. I'll check with them both." Grace scanned the room. "You've all been busy. It must be nice to get away with your friends and have fun. No stress."

The excitement in Brenda's eyes faded. "Yeah, lots of fun."

"Did you enjoy your class?" Grace asked after a moment.

Brenda nodded, and then she burst into tears.

Grace put down her trash bag and came over to her side. "I could tell you were upset about something when I came in. Is there anything I can do for you?"

Brenda wiped at her eyes with a low, rueful laugh. "For a start, you can tell me where I can get some tissues."

Grace went to the sleek sideboard, opened a drawer, and took out a small box of tissues. She handed it to Brenda. "How's that?"

"Thank you." Brenda blotted her eyes and blew her nose. "Sorry for being so stupid."

Grace sat next to her again, only kindness in her eyes. "Being upset is not the same thing as being stupid, you know."

"No, stupid is doing the same thing over and over and expecting different results. Oh, wait. That's insanity, isn't it?"

Grace reached over and took her hand. "Would you like to talk about it? I'm a good listener."

Brenda took another shaky breath and then straightened her shoulders. "I'm sure you have better things to do than listen to a tedious story."

"I don't believe it's tedious. If it's hurting you, then it's important, whatever it is."

Brenda felt the tears welling up again, but she blinked them back. "I guess you could tell as soon as Libby got here that she and I have a past."

"I thought that might be the case," Grace admitted.

"We're cousins. Libby's mother, Dot, and my mother were sisters. Their mother was our favorite grandmother. I never met Aunt Dot, but my mother always told me that she was kind of wild. Dot left school when she was sixteen and ran away with some guy. Grandma said it didn't matter. She was glad to have Libby stay with her all the time. We heard that Aunt Dot died several years ago."

Grace nodded sympathetically, waiting for Brenda to go on.

"Anyway, my mom and dad and I lived a couple of hours away from Grandma's, but every summer when school was out, I'd go and stay with her and Libby. She was older than me, but we were always best friends. We told each other everything, and if we really meant something, we'd say, 'Scout's honor.'"

Grace squeezed her hand.

Brenda laughed softly. "It was a silly thing to say. But still, we never said it unless we really meant it. We were so close, and now that's all gone."

"I don't mean to pry, but what happened between you and Libby?" Grace asked.

"I don't even understand how things fell apart so fast and over nothing. I think—" Brenda stopped and winced. "I know Libby was hurt because she didn't have the same kind of family I did. My parents were good to her, though. She and Grandma would come stay with us for Christmas, and we'd always make a big fuss over Libby's birthdays. But I know that's not the same as having your own mom and dad."

"That had to have been difficult for her," Grace murmured.

Brenda nodded but didn't say anything for a moment. Then she got the photo album out of her bag and opened it to the picture of her and Libby in the identical dresses. "Grandma made those dresses for us on a 1933 Featherweight. She claimed they were as good as store-bought ones, and it was true." She turned to the picture of her grandma behind her sewing machine. "She was so proud of that Featherweight. She taught Libby and me both to sew on it."

Grace smiled. "It's a beautiful machine."

"Featherweights haven't been made since the late '60s. They're still wonderful machines, so quilters snatch them up when they find a nice one for sale. Anyway, Grandma's . . ." Brenda bit her lip. "This sounds ridiculous. It's only a sewing machine, right?"

"Obviously, it meant a lot more," Grace told her.

Brenda drew a deep breath. "Grandma was good to Libby, and Libby was good to Grandma. Libby took care of Grandma when she got older. My mother had always had health problems, so when I grew up, I took care of her. That made it hard for me to visit Grandma and Libby as much as I would have liked to, but we stayed in touch by phone."

"That doesn't sound so bad," Grace said.

"I didn't think so. Libby didn't think so. Or at least that's what she told me at the time. Grandma died three years ago, and she left everything to Libby, which was fine with me. Libby had spent her whole life with her, and Grandma didn't have much besides her little house—the house Libby still lives in—and what was inside it."

Grace waited silently for Brenda to continue.

Brenda stared at the picture of her grandmother with the sewing machine, then jerked her head before a tear fell on it. "The only thing Grandma wanted me to have was the Featherweight."

"And your cousin wanted it too?" Grace asked gently.

"Libby always wanted everything. She always got everything. Mom and Dad told me to let her have her way because she didn't have parents of her own. I understood that. Most of the time, I didn't mind."

Grace nodded.

Brenda could feel the touch of bitterness in her smile. "I found out pretty quick that you either did things the way Libby wanted or you weren't her friend. Well, at that point I didn't care. She was my grandma too, wasn't she? Shouldn't I have at least one thing of hers? Just one? The one thing she wanted me to have?"

"I'm sure your grandmother knew you loved that sewing machine."

"I almost caved in and gave the Featherweight to Libby right then and there. But she was so nasty to me that I took it and left." Brenda shook her head. "When I got home, I tried to call her, but she wouldn't talk to me."

"Have you spoken to Libby since then?" Grace asked.

"No. She won't answer my phone calls, and she returns my letters unopened. I was hoping I might get a chance to talk to her here because we're going to be in close quarters for a week. I don't know what to say, except I'm sorry we aren't friends anymore. But am I supposed to be sorry for taking the one thing Grandma wanted me to have after she gave Libby everything else?"

"Is the sewing machine more important than your cousin?" Grace asked.

"Of course not. But when do I stand up for myself?"

"I'm sorry," Grace said. "It must be very difficult for you."

Brenda looked down at her album again, tracing one finger over a picture of herself and Libby and Grandma in the backyard planting irises. "The hardest part was when my mother died eighteen months ago. I thought Libby loved her, but when she and I had our argument, she cut off my whole family too. Mom had been sick for a long time, but even though I knew it was coming, I wasn't completely prepared for it."

Grace nodded in sympathy.

"I thought Libby would attend her funeral, and I hoped that she and I might even make up. I decided to give her Grandma's sewing machine too. I used a friend's phone to call her, because I knew she wouldn't answer a call from my number. Before she could hang up on me, I told her Mom had passed away and when the funeral was. I said I wanted things to be better between us. When I finished, she asked me if that was all I wanted to tell her, and I said yes. She hung up, and that was the end of it."

"And she didn't come to the funeral."

"No, she didn't." Brenda took a deep breath and forced herself to smile. "It sounds so stupid, doesn't it?"

"It sounds very painful," Grace said. "For both of you."

"My father died before my mother, so Libby is the only family I have left. And I'm the only family she has left. I wish there was a way I could fix what's gone wrong between us. But how do I do that without letting her run everything again?" Brenda let out a heavy breath. "I don't know what to do, but I'm afraid that coming here was a huge mistake."

"I'm not sure about that," Grace said. "Perhaps the best thing to do is exactly what you've been doing. Be willing to talk to Libby if she wants to talk. Be kind. Have a good time with your friends no matter what she does. Don't let her get to you."

"But what about the sewing machine?" Brenda asked.

"Your grandmother wanted you to have it. What you do with it now is something only you can decide." Grace smiled and stood up. "But you don't have to make a decision right this minute. At least have lunch first."

Brenda stood up too. "Thanks for letting me tell you all that. I didn't mean to keep you so long."

"Not a problem," Grace said. "It was nice to sit down for a minute. But I need to get back to work, and you'd better go have lunch before all the food is gone."

Brenda thanked her again and then walked out to the veranda where everyone was already filling their plates.

Libby sat next to Debbie. She gave Brenda a challenging look, obviously daring her to take the empty seat on her other side.

Brenda smiled at her and took the dare.

Robin

Robin had to admit that her mother had been right about coming to Magnolia Harbor. It was a beautiful place, especially now when the sun was dropping low in the sky, making the shadows long and distinct.

After drawing the gorgeous scene, she frowned at her sketch pad. The magnolia tree in the yard had graceful limbs and thick leaves, but the one she'd sketched resembled the famous Christmas tree Charlie Brown had brought home. She'd drawn plenty of trees before. Why couldn't she capture this one?

"Utter garbage," she muttered to the dog who was lounging beside her.

Winston smiled and wagged his tail.

He seemed to have no problem with it, but who was the artist here?

Robin poked around in her bag until she found her big eraser, then eliminated the magnolia tree. As she sketched the tree once more, she paid closer attention to the way the light hit the leaves and exactly how the shadows fell. It was better this time.

She examined the rest of the sketch. The lake was good, and she liked the way the sky had turned out. It looked as if you could reach into the page and push aside the clouds. But there was still something generic about the picture that contained a lake, a few trees, and the sky. It needed something more.

As Robin turned her attention to the lake, she noticed two children playing along the shore. Earlier, Robin had seen the little boy and girl with a man she assumed was their father. Now the man was nowhere in sight. He'd probably be back in a minute. The boy took his plastic pail and began packing it with sand. The girl joined him. Between the two of them, it took only a few minutes for a castle with four sturdy turrets to appear near the lapping water.

Robin glanced up at the sky. The light would be fading soon. She hadn't yet seen the children's mother, but the boy was no more than five years old, the girl possibly a year or two older. The father or someone had to be nearby, and it was pretty certain that whoever it was would be taking the children home for dinner soon.

There was no time to waste. She began to draw more quickly to help her remember the scene. She added a line here and there, the angle of an arm or a leg, the tilt of a head, the curve of a laughing mouth. Children moved so fast. Then they were gone.

She sketched in the girl's hair but immediately erased it. There wasn't the slightest bit of curl in the honey-colored locks. Her hair was perfectly straight and shining. It was a waterfall hanging down, hiding her face as she molded the sand with surprising dexterity. She was using a stick to make crenellations in the top of her castle walls.

The boy had dark hair that curled at the back of his neck, and his lithe limbs appeared round and sturdy as he carried buckets of sand to his sister at the construction site.

Seeing the kids reminded Robin of how she and Jason had wanted to have their own children someday. Before her thoughts could continue down that path, she stopped them. These cute kids on the beach would make a good picture. That was all.

Robin put in more details, such as the girl's upturned nose, the dimple in the boy's cheek when he laughed, the seahorse on the side of his pail. It was the little things that made a picture come alive. She added the scrape on the girl's knee and the pink ruffle around the hips of her one-piece bathing suit.

The light was fading fast now. She tried to work a little faster, knowing she could finish the picture in her room later as long as she got down enough details to capture the memory of how it had appeared.

"That's good."

Her pencil jerked, spoiling the line of the boy's calf, and she twisted to see the children's father peeking over her shoulder. He had traded his swim trunks for jeans and a T-shirt, and he carried a couple of towels.

"Sorry," the man said with a tentative smile. "I didn't mean to startle you."

"Oh, that's okay." Robin guessed the man was divorced, since she hadn't seen his wife anywhere. He most likely had the kids for a few days before they went back to their mother. He was probably trying to pick up the woman alone by the lake. She supposed the man was attractive enough, with his dark hair curling at the back of his neck just like his son's, but it didn't matter. She wasn't interested in meeting anybody.

"That picture is very good," he went on. "Do you think I could buy it from you?"

"I'm sorry, but no," Robin said. "It's not nearly finished, and I don't sell my work. It's more of a hobby than anything."

"No, I'm sorry." The man smiled a little more and shifted the towels into his right hand, exposing the gold band on the third finger of his left. "They grow up so fast, and I thought it would be great to have something like that to remember the moment."

So he was married. Well, that might be all right. If he was the nice guy he seemed to be, then Robin didn't have to worry about him wanting to go out with her. If he wasn't, then she had no trouble letting him know what she thought of cheaters, especially when there were children involved.

Robin let her expression soften, if only a little. "That's true, isn't it? They're adorable kids."

His blue eyes lit up. “I agree, but I might be a bit prejudiced. Oh, my name’s Rick Collins. The kids are Katie and Will.”

“I’m Robin.” She didn’t see the need to give him her last name.

“And your friend?” Rick asked, motioning to the dog sitting next to her.

“That’s Winston,” she answered. “He’s an ideal companion, but unfortunately he’s not mine. He lives at the Magnolia Harbor Inn, where I’m staying.”

Hearing his name, Winston jumped to his feet and gave a doggy grin.

Rick leaned down and petted the dog. “Winston, it’s my pleasure.”

Winston wagged his tail, obviously excited to make a new friend.

“Are you sure you won’t change your mind about the picture?” Rick asked. “I promise I won’t quibble about the price.”

“No, I’m not worried about that. I mean, it’s not much more than a sketch.” She frowned, thinking. “What if I try to finish it up, and then you can decide if you really want it? Are you going to be at the lake long?” She knew that they couldn’t be staying at the Magnolia Harbor Inn. Mom’s quilting friends were packed in there.

“We’re staying at The Tidewater for the week,” he said and nodded toward the lights on the other side of the lake. “Do you think you might be ready for me to take a look by, say, Friday?”

“I think so,” Robin said.

“Thank you,” Rick said. “I’ve seen you out sketching a couple of times. The kids haven’t bothered you or anything, have they?”

She shook her head. “I hope you don’t mind me drawing them. They fit the picture so well that I couldn’t help myself.”

“Not at all,” Rick said, then turned. “Hey, kids, come here a second.”

“But you didn’t see the castle,” Will protested as he and his sister stood up from their work.

"I can see it from here," Rick told them. "It looks great, but you should come see this."

The children slowly approached. They glanced at Robin and Winston.

"Can we pet your dog?" Katie asked.

"He's not mine," Robin said. "But he's very friendly, and I'm sure he won't mind. His name is Winston."

Katie and Will lavished attention on Winston, and the dog yipped and danced around their feet.

"I want you to meet Miss Robin and see what she's been doing," Rick said to his children.

After Robin greeted the kids, she showed them her drawing.

"That's us!" Will said, his eyes widening.

Katie grinned, revealing a missing lower tooth. "How did you do that?"

"I just drew it," Robin said. "Do you like it?"

The girl nodded. "Can you show me how?"

"That might take some time," Robin admitted. "When you go home, maybe your daddy can find someone who can teach you."

"But we'll be here the whole week," Katie said. "I can learn a lot in a week."

"Now, Katie," her father chided gently. "Miss Robin has things she needs to do, and she doesn't have time to give art lessons to little girls who can't even say please."

Katie ducked her head.

"I would like to learn to draw too, please, Miss Robin," Will said, turning his big blue eyes up to her.

She couldn't help but smile. "Well, maybe I could give you a lesson next time you're out here."

"Tomorrow?" Katie asked eagerly. "Please?"

Rick shook his head, more indulgent than censuring. "See what I have to deal with every day? But don't let them talk you into something you don't want to do."

Somehow Robin felt as if she wanted to do it, but she might feel differently tomorrow. After all, what did she know about teaching children how to draw? Still, it might be fun to try. She'd been here only two days, and she was already bored out of her mind. Maybe a few simple art lessons would be a good way to get her mind off herself. If the lessons ended up being hard to deal with, she could always tell them she was too busy to continue.

"I suppose we could give it a try." Robin smiled at Katie and Will. "What do you think? Can you be here around ten o'clock?" It would provide them enough time to draw before lunch, and it would still give her the early part of the morning alone.

"Only if you're sure you don't mind," Rick said to Robin. "These two can be a handful."

"Terrifying, I'm sure," Robin replied.

Will seemed dismayed. "We'll be good. Promise."

"I know you will," Robin assured him.

"Can you bring Winston too?" Katie asked as she hugged the dog.

"I'll see if he wants to come," Robin answered. "Now, you'd better go have your dinner. I have to get cleaned up so I can have mine too."

"Come on," Rick said to the kids, then addressed Robin. "We'll be back at ten. Thank you."

When they were gone, she sighed and scratched behind Winston's ears. "What did I just agree to?"

Winston stared at her but offered no advice.

"Katie and Will don't seem like they'd be any trouble, and their dad appears to be a nice guy—nothing like the predatory jerks I've met before, though those don't seem to exist around here. Still, what am I going to teach those kids to draw? Stick figures?"

Winston smiled and wagged his tail.

"Robin?"

She glanced toward the inn. Her mother was calling her from the veranda. It was time for dinner. Maybe she'd eat in their room again so she wouldn't have to listen to all the excited chatter from Mom and her friends. She packed up her pencils, tucked her sketch pad under her arm, and hurried up to where Mom was waiting.

Winston followed as fast as his little legs could carry him.

"How did it go?" Mom asked in her overly casual voice. "Can I see?"

"I ran out of good light." Robin showed her the sketch of the two kids and the lake.

"That's great," her mom said, then leaned down to pet Winston. "I saw you talking to the family. Are they staying nearby?"

Robin nodded. "At The Tidewater across the lake. I don't know much about them, though." *So don't ask me about the guy*, she added to herself. *He's taken, and I'm not interested anyway.* "I thought they'd look good in the picture."

"They certainly do," Mom said, then paused. "I've been meaning to tell you about the hatbox on the reception desk. Grace told me that you're welcome to use it."

"What is it for?" Robin asked.

"Sometimes guests write notes about the things they're dealing with and leave them in the box," Mom explained. "In return, they receive advice or encouragement."

Robin couldn't imagine relating details about her personal life to a stranger. Even in a note. "I don't know . . ."

"Grace said you can be anonymous," her mother added. "It might help to write down your feelings. Will you at least consider it?"

Knowing that her mother was only trying to help, Robin nodded.

"So how about dinner?" Mom asked. "Remember that chicken spaghetti recipe you liked so much? Ellen made a casserole with it, and I heard it's delicious."

"Sure, I guess."

"And there's garlic bread. I know you like that."

"Yeah, it sounds good," Robin said. "I'll get a plate to take up to our room."

"That'll be fine." Her mother almost managed to keep her disappointment from showing.

Maybe it wouldn't be such a bad idea to stay and eat with everyone else. It would certainly make Mom happy, and the other ladies were all friendly without being pushy. Robin had known most of them as long as her mother had, so she didn't feel too much like a stranger around them.

"On second thought, I think I will join you and your friends," Robin said.

Mom smiled. "I'm so glad."

When Winston took off for the kitchen, Robin followed her mother to the veranda and got in line behind her at the food table.

"You're not going to hide from us again tonight, are you?" Wanda called out from a nearby table.

Robin stopped filling her plate and turned to Wanda. The older woman had made a huge bow with cartoon ducks on it, and it was perched jauntily in her flaming-red hair. Robin had to force herself not to laugh.

"You can sit by us," Frankie said, patting the empty chair between her and Wanda.

There was something about Frankie's fluffy white curls and her merry face that always made Robin think of Mrs. Claus. It was hard to say no to Santa's wife. "If you're sure there's room."

"There's always room," Frankie insisted.

Robin smiled and walked over to the women.

"Sit right here," Wanda said, taking Robin's plate and setting it down on the table. She waved to Robin's mother. "You too. You can see pictures of my family, including Linnet, my new great-granddaughter."

"That's a pretty name," Robin said. "How many do you have now?"

Wanda removed a photo album from her purse and handed it to Robin. "Grands or great-grands?"

"Both," Robin answered as she opened the album.

Wanda thought for a moment. "Seventeen grandchildren and eight great-grandchildren. And one of the greats will be getting married next spring, so I expect I'll have at least one great-great before I'm done."

"That's amazing," Robin said, flipping through the pictures. "I'll bet you've had a wonderful life."

"Still having it." Wanda grinned at her. "I'm not planning on quitting anytime soon."

Robin smiled wanly. It must be nice to have everything go your way all your life.

Wanda must have caught something in her expression, because she leaned a little closer and lowered her voice. "You know, honey, I've buried two husbands."

"I'm sorry," Robin said, startled.

"When I was younger than you are now, the first one went to Vietnam and never came back. I thought I'd never love anybody ever again. Then I met my second, and he was persistent. I kept telling him I wasn't interested in getting married again, right up to the day we eloped and ran off to Italy. I spent over forty years wandering the world with him. It was an awful thing when I didn't have him with me anymore."

There was a sudden ache in Robin's heart. It had been so hard to lose Jason, and they hadn't even been married yet. "It must be difficult being alone."

"Who says I'm alone?" Wanda asked. "My third husband is waiting for me at home. He's probably eating fast food because he's too stubborn to learn to cook." She chuckled. "I'll tell you what. It's quite an adjustment to marry a younger man."

Robin stared down at her plate, knowing her eyes had gone wide. "I suppose."

"Yeah," Wanda said, gently nudging her with an elbow. "He won't even be eighty until next year."

Robin couldn't help but giggle at the mischief in Wanda's eyes.

"That's better," Wanda said, smiling. "Now you eat that. I don't like to see food wasted."

When all the ladies were seated, they started talking about the charity quilt the group was making and the class they were going to have the next day.

Robin was content to eat her tasty dinner and consider what she was going to do for tomorrow's art lesson with Katie and Will.

Maybe a little socializing wasn't going to be that hard after all.

Debbie

With everyone helping, cleaning up after dinner took only a few minutes, but to Debbie, it felt like an eternity. She needed to go upstairs. She wouldn't make it through the evening if she didn't.

"Oh," Debbie said as everyone was heading toward the dining room to resume their quilting, "I think I left my glasses in my room. I'd better get them."

"They're not in your pocket?" Libby asked. "You usually keep them in your pocket."

"You had them on when you were sewing," Kathleen reminded her.

Debbie patted her pocket, feeling the plastic frames against her hip, and shook her head. "I think I must have left them by the sink before I came downstairs for dinner. I won't be a minute."

She forced herself to walk casually until she was out of sight of the foyer, and then she quickened her pace and hurried upstairs to the second floor. After glancing around the hallway to make sure she was alone, she slipped into the suite Tess was sharing with Brenda and Jessica.

Tess had gone through shoulder surgery some time ago, and she was doing well. Debbie knew her friend had brought her pain medication with her just in case she needed it. Maybe Tess didn't need the pills, but Debbie certainly did.

She'd been in the suite earlier in the day, scouting it out to see where Tess kept her medication. Debbie had brought some pills with her, but she always tried to plan ahead, to seek out opportunities, to be ready when any chance presented itself. Many of her friends took a little something for their pain. They'd had surgery or needed it, so she could usually take a few pills from one of them, a few more from another, without anyone noticing they were gone.

Debbie hated stealing from the friends she dearly loved. She wasn't a thief... except she was. But what else could she do? Her own doctor wouldn't give her more prescriptions, and she didn't want to insist. He couldn't know about this.

She suspected her other doctor, her women's specialist, did know or at least suspect. Debbie had gotten her to refill her prescription once, claiming her general practitioner had been out of town and his staff had gotten her orders mixed up. Debbie was afraid to use that story again.

With another glance at the door, Debbie crept into the bathroom and zeroed in on the group of prescription bottles on the counter next to the sink. She already knew which one she wanted. She wrenched open the bottle. It was about half full. If it had been full, a tablet or two more or less wouldn't be noticed. As it was, she was running a risk by taking any of them.

Against her better judgment, she tapped several pills out into her palm, her heart beating slightly faster as she examined them. After Debbie dropped all but one into her pocket, the same pocket that held her glasses that she hadn't forgotten in her room, she turned on the tap and filled her cupped hand with water. Then she swallowed the pill and wiped her hands on the towel on the rack.

Relief began to sweep over her. She could make it through the evening now.

Debbie turned on the water again and rinsed her face, hoping she didn't look too bad. She'd be okay for a little while, but she needed to go to bed fairly early tonight.

She flipped off the light in the bathroom and the one near the door to the hall. Then she opened the door a crack and peeked into the hallway. Voices and laughter wafted up from the main floor, but there wasn't a sound upstairs.

The coast was clear, so Debbie slipped into the corridor and shut the door behind her with the tiniest of clicks. She assured herself that everything was all right.

When she reached the stairs, she turned and scanned the hall to make sure no one else was around. It was empty. She turned again and almost ran into Robin.

"I'm sorry," Robin said, picking up the pencil box she had dropped. "I didn't see you there."

"I didn't see you either," Debbie said, smiling brightly. "I hope I didn't break anything."

Robin jostled the box, making it rattle. "No, it's fine. It sounds like everything is still intact. Oh, I think they're looking for you downstairs."

"We're working on a charity quilt," Debbie explained. "There's a children's home not far from where we have our guild meetings, and we make quilts for all the kids every year. It's hard for some of them to be moved around, sometimes from home to home, and we like to give the children something they can keep for their very own."

"That's nice. Well, I hope you all have fun. I'm going up to my room to read." Robin smiled shyly, then headed toward the stairs that led to her third-floor suite.

Debbie stood there for a few seconds more, letting her racing heart slow. Robin hadn't seen anything, had she? Surely not. She hadn't made it to the top of the stairs before Debbie had shut the door to Tess's suite. And even if Robin had seen Debbie coming out of that room, she wouldn't think anything of it. She had no way of knowing whose room was whose. She and her mother weren't even staying on this floor.

No, it was okay. Everything was fine.

After Debbie calmed down, she started descending the sweeping staircase to the foyer. She stopped abruptly when she saw Winnie walking through the front door.

Debbie hurried down the remaining stairs and greeted her friend with a hug. "I didn't expect to see you back so soon."

"I came to drop off something," Winnie said. She narrowed her eyes as she studied Debbie. "Are you feeling all right? You aren't doing too much, are you?"

"I'm fine." Debbie laughed softly and leaned closer. "Don't tell anybody, but I might be too old to stay up so late anymore."

"There you are." Libby emerged from the dining room, a partly sewn quilt block and a pattern page in her hands, and made a beeline for Debbie. "Have you gone over this pattern? I don't think the measurements are correct."

"Actually, I haven't used that one before." Debbie managed a thin smile. "I thought it would be good for the kids' quilts we're making. Nice and simple, you know?"

"Not if it doesn't fit together," Libby snapped. "You'd better check it."

Debbie kept the smile plastered to her face. She was afraid that a single pill wasn't going to be enough, but she didn't dare take another one in front of everybody.

Winnie was looking at her strangely. "Are you sure you're feeling all right?"

"It's nothing. I just have a headache," Debbie replied. "But I'll go back upstairs and get something for it."

"What about this pattern?" Libby demanded, waving the page around. "We can't get much done if the whole pattern is wrong."

"Give me a minute," Debbie said, her expression placid. "Have you all chosen the fabrics you want to use?"

Libby nodded.

"I have some aspirin that really works for me," Winnie said, digging in her purse.

"Oh no, I don't want to take yours," Debbie said. "I have plenty upstairs."

"Here you go." Winnie pressed two of the white tablets into Debbie's palm. "You take those and see if they don't help."

Debbie forced another smile. "Thank you. I'll take them when I get back to the dining room. I have a bottle of water in there."

"Good," Libby said, thrusting the pattern page and the quilt block toward her. "Now you can tell us how we're supposed to make a quilt out of this."

"Before you leave," Winnie said to Libby, "I have something for you."

"For me?" Libby asked, cocking her head.

Her eyes alight, Winnie nodded. "For you." She reached into her purse and pulled out a screwdriver about eight inches long. "I was thinking you might need it."

Libby took it from her, clearly baffled. "I, uh, that's very nice of you, but I'm not sure what I'm supposed to do with this. It's too big for my sewing machine, and I already have one that fits it perfectly." She tried to hand the screwdriver back.

Winnie patted her hand. "You go ahead and keep it for now. If it turns out that you don't find a use for it, then you can give it to one of my nieces before you leave. They'll return it to me."

Libby still seemed confused. "Well . . ."

"Hang on to it," Winnie insisted. "If it doesn't come in handy, then no harm done."

Debbie watched Libby. Sometimes it was hard to tell how her friend would react.

"I guess not," Libby said as she slipped the screwdriver into her bag. "If you need it back, let me know."

"I'll do that," Winnie responded.

For a moment, Libby looked at Winnie uncertainly, something she almost never did. "So you're teaching that class tomorrow on appliqué."

"Yes, and I haven't found any method I like as well," Winnie said. "It's amazing how accurate it is."

"I like the way I've been doing it," Libby said, a challenge in her voice. "I don't see any need to change."

"There are so many different ways to appliqué," Winnie said warmly. "If you've found a method that works for you, be sure to keep doing it. But many quilters have attempted it one way and didn't care for it, so maybe they'll benefit from learning a new technique. You never know until you try, right?"

"Well, sure," Libby said, sounding a bit deflated. "People have to do it whatever way they enjoy most."

"Exactly," Winnie said. "I've found most ways have their own pros and cons, so it depends on what each quilter is most comfortable with."

"That's true," Debbie chimed in.

"I'd better get going now," Winnie said. "I only came by to drop that off. I'll be back tomorrow to give my demonstration. I hope you'll both come."

"Of course we will," Debbie said cheerfully.

"I don't know," Libby said. "I suppose I'll be in there sewing, no matter what else is going on."

"That's fine too." Winnie gave Debbie a quick hug. "Have a good time, but don't stay up too late tonight, okay? Be sure to get some sleep and take those pills."

"I definitely will," Debbie said.

"Good. I'll see you both tomorrow." Winnie waved at them, then went out the front door.

"Now," Libby pressed, "about this pattern—"

"You go on back to the dining room," Debbie interrupted. "I have to use the restroom and take these pills, but I'll join you in a minute."

Before Libby could protest any further, Debbie strode to the restroom. She locked the door behind her, then leaned against it.

A moment later, she bent over the sink, gulping down more water and then swallowing the pills.

Not the aspirin Winnie had given her. The stolen painkillers.

Bracing her hands on the countertop, she took a deep breath. She was all right now, and she could get through the evening without going crazy.

As Debbie turned to go, she caught sight of herself in the mirror. No wonder Winnie had been concerned about her. She appeared unsettled. She smoothed her hair and straightened the collar of her blouse.

Then she peered at herself in the mirror once again. There were specks on the glass. No, there were specks on her glasses. She wiped them clean with one of the hand towels by the sink.

She'd better hurry. Libby would come searching for her if she didn't return soon.

As Debbie left the bathroom and headed across the foyer, she noticed the hatbox on the corner of the reception desk. After glancing around, she darted over to the box and took off the lid.

There was a folded piece of paper on top of the others. On the outside of the piece of paper, someone had written: *If you don't know what to do . . .*

It wasn't addressed to Debbie, but surely it was meant for her.

She hadn't signed her own note, so whoever had responded wouldn't know whom to address it to. With another furtive glance toward the dining room, she unfolded the piece of paper.

> *Your true friends will be there for you if you let them know you need them. You can let them see your weaknesses. They won't abandon you.*

Her eyes filled with tears as she read the words. Debbie wanted to believe the sentiment with her whole heart, but it wasn't possible. Not about this. Everyone thought she was a nice, middle-aged lady who went to church and made quilts for foster kids. But she was an addict. She was a thief. If they knew the truth, they wouldn't want anything to do with her.

"Please, God, help me," she breathed.

"I thought she was coming," Libby said from the dining room. "I'll go get her."

Debbie stuffed the note into her pocket with the rest of the pills she had stolen. Then she wiped the tears from her eyes, pasted on a smile, and strolled into the dining room.

Brenda

"I had to get a refill called in from my doctor," Tess remarked the next morning.

"Which prescription?" Brenda asked as she perused the various scraps of fabric she had spread out on the table in front of her. She was preparing her materials for today's appliqué lesson.

"My pain medication. My shoulder was bothering me last night after I cut all those two-and-a-half-inch strips for binding the kids' quilts. I thought I had enough pills left for the week if I needed them, but I'm nearly out. And it wasn't easy getting my doctor to refill my prescription."

Brenda glanced at her friend. "Why not?"

"I told the nurse I must have miscounted when I packed, but I got a pretty good lecture from her about not expecting to get another early refill after this." Tess rolled her eyes. "What do they think I'm doing with them? Selling them on street corners?"

"They have to be careful," Brenda answered, pulling out an old-fashioned rose-colored fabric and setting it aside. "So many people are addicted to painkillers now. It's an epidemic."

Tess huffed. "Well, not me. I didn't even take many pills right after my surgery. I only take them now when I've overused my shoulder or slept wrong or something. It's not fair for me to be treated like a criminal."

"I'm sure they only want to keep you from having a problem with them," Brenda said.

"I know," Tess said. "I put the bottle in my purse today, just in case I needed another one while we were down here, but that doesn't mean I'm going to take a handful of them."

Brenda placed an ivory fabric next to the rose-colored one.

Tess eyed the fabrics Brenda had chosen. "Is that for the appliqué demo today?"

Brenda nodded. "My grandmother made a quilt years ago. It had roses and daisies and all kinds of other flowers appliquéd on it. We used it for a picnic blanket and a play tent and whatever else we imagined. I hope to make one like it."

"Do you have a picture of your grandmother's quilt?" Tess asked.

Brenda dug the photo album out of her bag, turned to a picture of Grandma holding up the quilt, and showed it to her friend.

"It's pretty," Tess said.

"Isn't it?" Brenda asked. "Too bad the picture is faded. The real thing was very colorful."

"What are you talking about?" Ginny said from the table behind them. "I want to see."

Ginny and Jessica came over to look at the picture and then passed the album over to the next table.

Brenda winced when it reached Libby. Then she forced a smile. "Remember that one?" she asked her cousin. "Grandma was so proud of it. I don't know why she let us drag it everywhere when we were playing."

"You're going to make one like it?" Libby asked coolly. She had all but ignored Brenda at dinner the night before.

"I'd like to see how close I can get to the original," Brenda replied. "I was wondering if this new appliqué method we're supposed to learn would work for it."

"Grandma never did things in any fancy kind of way," Libby said dismissively. "She taught me the method she always used, and that's the only one I'm planning to follow." She pushed the album toward Brenda. "It looks like it worked for her."

"She was a much better quilter than I am," Brenda said, feeling her face heat.

Libby snorted derisively.

"Oh, that's gorgeous," Debbie said, studying the picture. "Your grandmother must have been extremely talented. It would take forever to finish something like that."

"I hope not," Brenda said.

"Well, you can work on it till you're eighty, but you'll never turn out anything as good as hers." Libby's pale-green eyes were diamond hard. "I'm surprised you didn't bring that Featherweight to sew it on since you think you're going to be Grandma and everything."

"I'm not trying to be her," Brenda said, trying to keep her voice steady and her expression calm. "And, yes, I know I'll never be as good as Grandma was, but I loved that quilt. I think you did too."

Libby scoffed.

"And I'm not using the Featherweight right now because I don't want it to get banged up moving it around all the time."

"You just didn't want me to see it." Libby's heavy brows were drawn together, her thin lips pursed. "I hope you're proud of yourself."

Tess gave her a reproachful look. "Now, Libby—"

"Don't you start with me, Tess Harrison," Libby warned, cutting her off. "Brenda knows it as well as I do. Look at her hanging her head like the thief she is, taking what should have been mine."

Tess chuckled.

Brenda stared at Tess. She didn't know how her friend managed to laugh right in front of Libby. But there was nothing derisive about her laughter. It was warm and full of good-natured humor.

"Goodness, you'd think you didn't get every last bit of your grandmother's things besides that sewing machine," Tess said. "Shouldn't Brenda have gotten something of hers, especially if that's what your grandma wanted?"

Wanda peered over her sewing machine with bright shining eyes, looking for all the world like a baby bird with sparse red pinfeathers. "You ought to get back to your sewing, Lib," she said dryly. "People are going to think you don't know when you're talking nonsense."

Libby scowled at her and dropped back into her chair with a huff, immediately bending over her machine and jamming her foot onto the pedal, making the motor roar.

Debbie smiled weakly. "Well, who wouldn't want a Featherweight, right? But I think you have the nicest machine here, Libby. All those amazing features, and—" She broke off, obviously realizing that Libby wasn't paying the least bit of attention to her, and changed the subject. "Winnie ought to be here for our demonstration soon."

Brenda checked her watch. Debbie was correct. It was nearly time. "I'm looking forward to seeing the antique quilts too."

A few minutes later, Winnie entered the dining room followed by Grace and a tall, good-looking man of fifty or so with his arms full of quilts.

The gathered quilters stopped what they were doing and gave the newcomers their undivided attention.

"Good morning," Winnie said. "It's time for a special treat. Is everyone here?"

Debbie scanned the room. "Yes, we're all here."

"First off," Winnie said, "I'd like to introduce Spencer Lewis. He's the owner of the nearby Blossom Hill Farm, and he grows the most delicious pecans you've ever tasted."

The group greeted him warmly, and Spencer smiled in return.

"Now, as Spencer will tell you, he doesn't know a lot about quilts," Winnie said. "But he would like to say a few words about his great-grandmother who made them."

"My great-grandmother on my father's side was born in 1882," Spencer said. "She had ten children, and I couldn't tell you how many grandchildren and great-grandchildren. My father remembers that she had a quilt frame that was pulled up to the dining room ceiling when she wasn't using it. He said she carded her own cotton for batting and cut out pieces of cardboard from cereal boxes to make the templates she used." He turned to Winnie. "I'll let Winnie talk about the quilts themselves."

Brenda leaned forward in her chair, eager to see the quilts.

"Thank you, Spencer," Winnie said. "Now if you and Grace would be kind enough to show the quilts as I'm talking about them, I'd appreciate it."

Brenda smiled as she watched Spencer and Grace wrangling the quilts. Unless she was mistaken, there was a spark of something between them. She thought they'd make a nice couple.

Winnie spent the next few minutes describing the fabrics and techniques quilters used in the early part of the twentieth century. Her two helpers held up the quilts as she discussed them.

Several of the ladies asked questions, and afterward they all left their seats to take a closer look.

"Your great-grandmother's stitches are beautiful," Frankie told Spencer. "They're so small and even."

"Good thing she was the quilter and not me," Spencer joked. "They'd have ended up being made out of fishing line and duct tape."

Brenda laughed. "My grandmother had a quilt like this one." She pointed out the quilt that had been appliquéd with little girls in pretty sunbonnets. "I'm sure it's long gone by now, but I remember it fondly."

Libby sidled up next to her. "I guess if you'd been around more, you'd have known all about Grandma's things. But don't let that bother you."

"Libby—" Brenda said.

"It's time for our appliqué lesson," Libby interrupted. With a saccharine smile, she returned to her seat.

Brenda ducked her head, knowing everyone had overheard.

Tess gave her a small, understanding smile and sat down again.

Not for the first time, Brenda felt grateful for Tess. It would have been impossible to get through this retreat without her. She always seemed to be able to diffuse a tense situation. Still, she couldn't have Tess with her every minute of every day. And what about after the retreat?

Winnie and the others thanked Grace and Spencer, and the two left with the quilts. Then Winnie began telling them about prepared-edge appliqué.

Brenda tried to focus on the session. She didn't dare glance at Libby. With the way Libby had rejected all of Brenda's attempts to reconcile, Brenda feared that her cousin had already made up her mind.

Maybe some broken relationships could never be mended.

10

Debbie

Except for the nearly constant whir of Libby's sewing machine, the room was quiet. Winnie's demonstration of her appliqué method was a hit with all the ladies who had tried it, and now they sat over their practice projects utilizing their new skills.

Working with an iron and some liquid starch, Debbie tried her best to remember everything Winnie had said. It would have been easier if she didn't feel so sick, but she couldn't take another pill yet. She had to get through the rest of the week on what she had.

"This is amazing," Ellen said, showing her neighbors the leaf she had just turned. "Perfect points, smooth curves. It's gorgeous and not hard at all."

Amanda frowned. "I can't get this bump out of the side of mine."

"Did you cut your template correctly?" her sister asked. "Winnie said that any irregularities in your template are going to show in your appliqué piece."

Debbie squeezed her eyes shut. Maybe she should go ahead and take another pill. She remembered the last time she had tried to quit. She didn't want to go through that again, especially in close quarters like this. Maybe she'd try to get off the painkillers when she returned home. Her dogs wouldn't notice if she didn't smile all the time.

As she regarded the mess she was making, she sighed. It was a simple circle, meant to be the center of a flower. There were noticeable tucks in the edge of the piece, and one side of the circle was decidedly straight. She needed to take a pill. If she was going to get through this, she had to have another one.

Suddenly realizing the sewing machine beside her had stopped, Debbie glanced up.

Libby smirked at her. "It's not such a great new method after all, is it?"

Debbie pulled the paper template out of the attempted circle and smiled apologetically. "I think it would be good if I could do it correctly. Winnie's sure looked pretty, and it was perfect." She rubbed her temple, letting the apology in her smile turn to discomfort. "If I didn't have such a headache, I would be able to do better with this."

"I don't see what's so special about that method," Libby argued. "The way I do it works just fine."

"Yes, you've made so many quilts with it. I can see why you wouldn't want to change." Debbie took off her glasses and massaged both temples. "I'm going upstairs to get some aspirin. I'll be right back."

"I have a bottle of aspirin with me," Libby said, scooping her purse off the floor and setting it on her lap. "You can take a couple of mine."

"Thanks, but I have a particular kind I use," Debbie said, keeping the wan smile on her face. "It won't take me more than a minute to go up and get some of those."

"Don't be silly." Libby removed a bottle from her purse, took out two tablets, and handed them to Debbie. "Mine are exactly the same kind. I saw yours by the sink. Go ahead. You can always give me a couple next time we're upstairs."

Debbie hesitated, scrambling for another excuse to go to their room. "You might need them for yourself. How's your knee been?"

"That's nothing," Libby said. "And if it gets bad, I have some stronger stuff I can take."

Debbie cringed inwardly. She had seen that bottle in their room. It had made her stomach lurch each time she passed by it, but she hadn't dared touch it. Libby would know, wouldn't she? It had been better to take some from Tess because she was so laid-back about everything. She was nothing like Libby. Debbie wished she could make the pills last the rest of the week, but she was afraid she wouldn't be able to.

If only Debbie could remain under control until she could take another pill. She should have put the medicine in her purse and kept it with her. It would have been easier to slip into the restroom on this floor. Maybe the other women wouldn't notice her going back upstairs now. Maybe—

"Go on and take those," Libby urged. "I want you to tell me what you think of the fabrics I picked for this block."

Debbie pretended to swallow the aspirin, but she slid them into her pocket instead. Then she took a couple of deep breaths and smiled again. She had to keep smiling. Otherwise, someone would know.

She checked out the fabrics Libby had chosen. They were soft, gentle florals, dots, and stripes. Libby was always great at coordinating fabrics for her quilts, even if her appliqué method could have used some improvement.

"What pretty fabrics," Debbie said as the pinks and blues and greens swirled in front of her eyes. "Are they from the same fabric line you used in the other blocks?"

"It's several different lines," Libby answered. "I don't like to stick with only one. What do you think?"

"I like it. Those pinks would be perfect for the roses. They're all . . ." Debbie's head swam, and she closed her eyes and took a deep breath.

"Debbie?" Libby said, and her voice sounded strange.

"Are you all right?" Brenda asked, approaching them.

Debbie managed to open her eyes. "I'm sorry, but I have an awful headache."

"I gave her some aspirin," Libby said.

"I need to go upstairs and rest for a little while." Debbie got to her feet. "I'll be back soon. Please keep sewing."

There was a general murmur of concern from the other ladies.

"Are you sure you don't need any help?" Carolyn asked.

Tess took Debbie's arm. "I'll go upstairs with her."

"No, that's all right." Debbie freed herself with a light laugh that wasn't entirely forced. "I'm okay. I'm just going to rest for a few minutes."

Tess walked Debbie to the door. "Feel better soon."

"I will," Debbie assured her, then went upstairs.

The hallway on the second floor was empty. It was the perfect opportunity to sneak out a few more of Tess's pills. Yes, she had a little more in her own room, but she could tell already that they wouldn't last her all week, and she might not have another opportunity like this, especially if Tess started to suspect.

She made a mental list of everyone who had come to the retreat. All the ladies were downstairs sewing, except for Robin. Where would she be? Probably drawing out by the lake or sequestered in her room on the third floor. Debbie thought she'd heard the innkeepers in the kitchen, talking and probably preparing the quilters' next meal. She had to make this quick anyway. If Robin happened to come down the hall again as Debbie was leaving a room she didn't belong in, she might ask uncomfortable questions.

Tess's door was unlocked. Debbie quickly opened it, entered the room, and shut the door. She hurried to the bathroom door. That door was not quite shut, and it creaked as she pushed it open. She glanced over her shoulder at the door to the hall, but nothing was stirring. Debbie shook her head, chiding herself for acting silly. No one could have heard the door creaking.

When she switched on the light, she couldn't help but moan. The bottle wasn't there.

She darted over to the sink and started picking up the other bottles. There was medicine for diabetes, cholesterol, and high blood pressure. Everything but what she needed.

Debbie wanted to cry. She couldn't believe that Tess had moved her supply. Did she know some of the pills had been stolen? Did she suspect Debbie? No, she couldn't know the truth.

She crept out of the suite and rushed to the room she shared with Libby. Debbie ran to the bathroom and opened the drawer she was using. At the back was a zippered pouch she had made in one of the classes she and all the other quilters had taken a few years ago. She kept her makeup brushes in it and the small plastic bag that held her pills.

Her hands shook as she opened the plastic bag and took out one precious tablet, but as she closed the bag, she fumbled the pill and watched in horror as it disappeared down the drain.

Now she did cry. She had so few painkillers left to make it through the rest of the retreat. She wouldn't be returning home for several days. When she got home, she'd figure out some way to get more medication, but it would be too awkward and risky to do it here.

She carried her bag out of the bathroom and over to the bed and removed another pill. Before she could drop this one, she put it into her mouth and swallowed it without water.

Clutching the bag against her heart, she closed her eyes and sank onto the bed. What was she going to do? What could she do?

She went back into the bathroom and opened one of the drawers Libby had taken for herself. Debbie had never been so bold as to go through Libby's belongings, but she didn't care now. Still, she was cautious as she picked up various pill bottles, examined them, and put them back exactly where they had been. Finally, she found the right bottle.

As Debbie opened the bottle, she laughed in relief to discover it was almost full. But she hesitated. If Libby found out that any of the pills were missing, wouldn't Debbie be the most likely suspect? After all, she and Libby were the only ones sharing this suite.

However, Tess and a few other members of the group were taking this kind of prescription right now. Wouldn't they be suspected first? Also, several more women had had some sort of surgery, and they had most likely been prescribed pain medication.

Before she could think about it anymore, she tapped the side of the bottle, letting a few of the pills fall into her hand. Then she jiggled the bottle and peered into it. Did it look any different? Different enough for Libby to notice? Maybe not. She hadn't taken that many.

Debbie returned the bottle to the drawer, put her stolen pills into the plastic bag, and slid the plastic bag into the zippered pouch.

Then she stretched out on the bed and closed her eyes.

11

Robin

"See?" Will held up his version of the bird Robin had taught him and his sister to draw.

"Wow. It's wonderful." Robin thought he had done a good job with the shape of the head and body and the position of the wings, but there was some sort of round object in the bird's claws that she didn't recognize. There was certainly nothing like that in her example.

Robin leaned forward in her beach chair. "What does it have?" she asked Will, pointing to the object in question. "It looks like it's carrying something."

Winston sat up as if inspecting the drawing too.

"She's a mommy bird, and that's her egg," Will answered, his blue eyes bright. "She's taking it with her when she goes to get worms."

Katie frowned as she examined her brother's picture. "Mommy birds don't take their eggs with them. They leave them in their nests."

Will's eager expression became suddenly anxious. "But then who will take care of the eggs when she's gone? What if something happens to her? Will the daddy come home and take care of them?"

"The daddy has to get worms too," Katie said. "They eat all the time."

"But that's after the babies are hatched," Robin told the children. "When they're still in their eggs, the mommy stays with them to keep them warm. After they hatch and get big enough, she helps the daddy get food for them."

"But what if the mommy doesn't come back?" Will asked, his chin quivering.

Rick had been dozing on a beach towel beside them, but now he raised himself up on one elbow. He took one look at his distressed son and immediately sat up. "Hey," he said softly, holding out his arms.

Will went to his dad.

"We talked about how God sees even the little birds and knows everything that happens to them, right?" Rick asked.

Will nodded.

"They'll be okay."

"But what if the mommy doesn't come back?" Will pressed.

"Then their daddy takes care of them," Rick replied.

"But what if he—"

"He always takes care of them," Rick said firmly, and then he gave Will a warm smile that crinkled the corners of his eyes. "Now both of you show me what you drew."

Will held up his drawing and described it again, this time without further comments from his sister.

Then Katie, hanging on her daddy's arm, displayed the pair of bluebirds she had drawn, both with copious musical notes coming from their beaks.

"Those are both great," Rick told them. "I think you've learned a lot today. Did you tell Miss Robin thank you?"

"Thank you, Miss Robin," the children chorused.

"You're both welcome," she said. "I had a good time too. And so did Winston."

The dog barked his agreement.

They all laughed.

Rick collected the drawings from the kids. "I'll take care of your pictures while you go have a quick swim, and then we have to leave. Hurry now."

With a squeal, Katie sprinted toward the lake. Will and Winston were right behind her, Winston barking the whole way.

"You know," Robin said when they were out of earshot, "sometimes male birds abandon their young if the female disappears."

"Only some of them," Rick said. "Others are the best dads ever. For example, take penguins. Male penguins often keep their eggs warm while their mates are off hunting, and they help parent the chick when it hatches."

"Okay," Robin said. "Apparently, you're the expert."

He shrugged. "So many people assume the worst about dads, but it's not always true."

"I know. I had a great dad." Robin felt the words choke up in her throat. Her father had been gone for a long time now. In many ways, Jason had reminded her of her dad. They were both men she could trust, who would love and protect her no matter what. She stopped her train of thought, not wanting to start crying in front of someone she hardly knew. "If you don't mind, I really don't want to go over the past. After all, it's done with, right?"

Rick nodded. "Anything before yesterday is off-limits. So, thanks for giving the kids an art lesson. They enjoyed their time with you." He grinned as he regarded Winston. "And that's a great dog."

"Isn't he?" She sighed dramatically. "But I don't think the ladies who own the inn are going to let me take him home."

"That's a shame." He studied her for a moment. "You're obviously a dog lover."

"I am," Robin said. "Well, I like most animals, at least the ones that aren't going to hurt me if I pet them."

Rick laughed softly. "How many pets do you have?"

"I don't have any at the moment," she said. "But I grew up with just about everything—dogs, cats, rabbits, turtles, birds, and fish. We even had a guinea pig."

"That's quite a menagerie," he commented with a grin. "Why don't you have any pets now?"

"I haven't had the time to take care of a pet lately," Robin said. "It wouldn't be fair to the animal." It wouldn't be right to adopt a pet of any kind if she couldn't give it the love it needed, and she wasn't sure if she had much to give.

"It is a big responsibility," Rick said. "I think you're smart to hold off on adopting a pet until you're ready."

"Maybe someday. It's not like I'm ruling it out or anything." Robin cringed, hating the way she sounded like she owed him an explanation, which she didn't.

Rick smiled. "It's nice you can spend some time with Winston while you're here. All the fun and none of the responsibilities. I think he's having a good time with the kids."

"I'm enjoying it too," she admitted. "I'm here with my mom's quilting group and, well, it's just not my thing. I was getting bored doing nothing."

He chuckled. "My mother's a quilter. I don't ever remember her not having something she was working on. When I went off to college, she made me one of those—oh, sorry. I almost forgot. The past is off-limits."

"You don't have to be so strict about it," Robin said. "Just no true confessions."

Rick crossed his long legs under him on the beach towel and propped his elbows on them. "She made me a quilt out of a bunch of my favorite old T-shirts. You know, different teams I played on and schools I went to, my favorite bands, places I'd been. It's pretty worn now, but I still have it."

"That's so thoughtful," Robin said. "It amazes me how my mom and her friends can take the most mismatched fabrics and fit them into something that works."

"It sounds like the quilts my mom makes for the kids," Rick said. "They love picking out the fabrics, and she always surprises them with what she creates. She comes up with some of the craziest combinations you've ever seen."

She waved one hand over her sketch pad and colored pencils. "I've studied all the theory behind using color and contrast and scale and everything else to get different effects, but the ladies seem to know instinctively how to put these quilts together. I don't know how they do it."

"I guess it's something you pick up over time," he said. "My mother made Will a quilt with dinosaurs and ice-cream cones on it last month. Weird, right? But he hasn't slept without it since."

Robin couldn't help but laugh at the unusual combination. "Those were the fabrics he picked out?"

"Yep, and somehow she made them work together." Rick cocked his head and smiled. "You ought to do that more often."

"What?" she asked warily.

"Laugh. It's nice."

Robin felt herself blush, so she stared down at her sketch pad. There was no use getting interested in a guy who was already taken. Besides, she didn't want to start dating someone anyway.

"Look, I'm not saying anything about the past or asking any questions," he said gently. "But it's written all over your face. Whatever it is you're dealing with, don't waste your life trying to go back. You can't do it, and it will only make you miserable."

Still staring down at her sketch pad, she toyed with a pencil and didn't say anything.

"And don't let whatever's in the past keep you from seeing what's here and now," Rick went on. "There's a time to deal with whatever is bothering you. I can't say how long a time that is for you or anybody, but when that time is done, you can't be afraid of going on. You can't be afraid of trying again." He ducked his head so he could see her face. "Okay, that's the end of the sermon."

Robin blinked and swallowed hard. Even though she'd been annoyed when she heard the same advice before, somehow it didn't bother her this time. She knew Rick was attempting to be kind, and she didn't want to be a total wet blanket, so she smiled and said, "Thanks. I'll keep that in mind."

"Good deal." He got to his feet, shading his eyes as he turned to gaze out at the lake. "I'd better get the kids. Mama will be waiting for us by now. Katie! Will!"

Katie grabbed her brother's hand, and the children ran back to their father with Winston trotting after them.

Rick handed the kids two towels from the tote bag they had brought along, and they started drying off.

Winston shook the water off himself, making the children giggle.

"Anyway, it was good of you to spend your time with the kids," Rick said to Robin. "We all enjoyed it, and Mama will like seeing their pictures."

"I was happy to do it," Robin said. "I never met a woman yet who didn't love her little ones' artwork."

"True. Well, come on, kids. It's time to go."

Will took his father's hand. "Are we still having a picnic tomorrow?"

Rick nodded. "Unless we spend so much time out here that we end up missing it."

Katie laughed.

"Can Miss Robin come with us?" Will asked, peeking at Robin from under his long lashes.

"She's welcome, of course," Rick said. "But she might have other things she needs to do. She has already spent a lot of time with both of you today."

"Please, Miss Robin?" Katie asked. "We won't make you help us draw again."

Robin smiled at her. "Thanks for the invitation, but I wouldn't want to intrude. I'm sure the four of you will have a wonderful picnic."

"No, it'll only be me and the kids," Rick said. "Mama's having lunch with a friend of hers. You're welcome to join us if you want to come."

"Please, Miss Robin," Will said. "We like you."

Katie nodded vigorously.

"Okay, if you're sure it won't be a bother," Robin said, smiling again. "Is there anything I can bring?"

"Just yourself." Rick smiled too. "There's a small picnic area near The Tidewater. You can't miss it once you're over there."

"I'll meet you there tomorrow at lunchtime," Robin said. "How's that?"

Will clapped. "Yay! Can Winston come?"

"I'm afraid not," Robin told him. "He belongs here at the inn, and I think he'd be missed. But I'll bet he would like it if you came back sometime to see him."

Winston yipped as if in agreement.

Everyone laughed.

Rick stuffed the towels into the tote, looped the bag over one arm, and then took the kids by the hand. "We'll see you tomorrow, Robin."

"Tomorrow," she said, waving as they walked away.

"Bye!" Katie called over her shoulder.

When they were gone, Robin knelt down to pat Winston's damp head. "I'm sure I'll never see them again after the retreat is over, but it'll be good to do something different for once, don't you think? And they're a nice family. Maybe I'll drop by The Tidewater sometime and meet the children's mom."

12

Brenda

"I can't do this anymore," Brenda muttered. She sat on the edge of the four-poster bed that dominated the Rosebud Suite. "Coming here was definitely a mistake. Libby and I haven't spoken in three years. Why should it be any different during the retreat?"

"It wasn't that bad, was it?" Tess sat down on the bed next to Brenda and put an arm around her. "Libby wasn't very nice about the sewing machine your grandmother willed to you. But it's not like the two of you had a shouting match or anything. And you saw how Libby backed down as soon as Wanda chimed in."

Brenda laughed faintly. "Wanda isn't the least bit intimidated by anybody."

"Especially Libby," Tess added. "And you shouldn't be either."

"It's not just about earlier today," Brenda said. "Dinner tonight was awful. Libby acted like I didn't even exist. It was so uncomfortable, and Debbie made it even worse by hovering around, trying to force everybody to be happy."

Tess sighed. "Debbie tries so hard. I've never seen anybody who wants to keep the peace more than she does. And Libby runs right over her."

"Exactly. I don't know why Debbie puts up with it. She'd get more respect if she stood up for herself and stopped letting everyone push her around all the time."

"People can't take advantage of you unless you let them," Tess said, peering at Brenda over her rhinestone glasses.

"And if you don't let them, they cut you off." Brenda winced, knowing her comment had come out with more bitterness than she intended. "How long am I supposed to keep trying?"

"Libby's your cousin, for goodness' sake," Tess said. "She's family."

"I guess I don't have any family anymore. Nobody but you."

Tess gave her a hug. "You know I love you and I'm happy to have you as part of my family, but Libby needs you too."

Brenda scoffed.

"I mean it," Tess insisted. "She's a handful to deal with and just plain mean sometimes, but she's really hurting. People don't react the way she has if they don't care."

"She's mad because I stood up to her for once. What am I supposed to do?" Tears welled up in Brenda's eyes, and she blinked them back. "She's always gotten her way. Every single time. And now that I want one thing for me, she throws a fit. I'm not doing it anymore."

"Do you think Libby will be friends with you again if you give her the sewing machine?" Tess asked.

"I'm not sure." Brenda reached over to the table beside the bed and plucked a tissue from the rose-covered box. "But if I let her push me around again, what kind of friendship is that?"

"I know it isn't easy." Tess was silent for a moment. "But you two had a very special relationship when you were growing up. I can't believe that sewing machine is more important than that."

"It's not. Of course it's not. I'd give it to Libby this minute if I thought it would solve the problem. But I don't want to be loved based on what I give someone."

"I'm not saying you have to sacrifice your self-esteem," Tess answered. "But what would it hurt to let her know you still love her and want to have a relationship with her?"

Brenda closed her eyes. She determined not to fall apart over this, not even in front of Tess. "Rejection hurts. A lot."

"It does," Tess murmured, taking Brenda's hand and squeezing it. "And I'm sorry this has been so awful for you. I'm not trying to tell you what to do. You're the only one who knows if it would be worse to keep trying while you're both here or to leave wondering what it might have been like if you had tried."

"I knew before we arrived that this was going to be painful," Brenda admitted. "But I thought we might start talking. I didn't expect we'd be best friends again overnight, but I hoped things would get better. Now I don't know if they ever will."

There was a knock on the door, and Jessica came in. She sat down on the rollaway bed near the window on the other side of the fireplace and pulled out her suitcase from underneath it. "Are you two coming downstairs?" she asked as she rummaged in her bag.

"Pretty soon," Brenda replied. "How's it going?"

"We're about to start hand-sewing the binding on the charity quilts we've made so far," Jessica said. "Wanda suggested we split up into teams and make it a competition to see which team finishes first."

"That will certainly give the ladies motivation to finish the quilts fast," Tess remarked with a grin.

Jessica nodded as she pulled out a lightweight sweater, then closed the suitcase and shoved it under the bed.

"Is it chilly downstairs?" Brenda asked.

"No, Debbie was cold, so I told her she could borrow my sweater," Jessica responded. "I don't think she's feeling very well."

"I've noticed," Tess said. "But you know how she is. Everything's fine or it's going to be. She must be freezing if she mentioned it."

"Anyway," Jessica said, standing up, "Libby wants to work on her own stuff, but if you two will come, we'll have three teams of four, one person on each side of three quilts. What do you say?"

Brenda and Tess exchanged glances.

Brenda knew how it would be. Everyone would be sewing and chatting, and Libby would be sitting behind her machine, looming over them like an enormous storm cloud.

Well, Libby could do what she wanted. The rest of them were here to have a good time.

Brenda stood and pulled Tess to her feet beside her. "I say let's do it."

13

Robin

"Lake Haven is beautiful no matter which side of the shore you're on." Robin polished off her chocolate chip cookie and sighed contentedly. "And if I eat anything else right now, I think I'd sink right into the water."

Katie giggled.

Will popped the last bite of cookie into his mouth. "I could eat another one."

"Enough sweets for one meal," Rick said.

Will gave him a playful pout in return.

"Thanks for inviting me," Robin said. "Though I think this was a lot nicer than your average picnic lunch."

Rick grinned. "The owner of The Tidewater is a gourmet chef, so even ham sandwiches, chips, and cookies are naturally the very best."

"It sounds like where I'm staying." Robin could see a glimpse of the Magnolia Harbor Inn across the lake. She mused how nice it would be to draw the view from here at night when the lights of the inn would be shining in the water along with the gleam of the moon and stars. "I don't know how the two ladies who own it do everything on their own."

"They must work really hard," Rick said.

"And even with the food we brought ourselves, they add a lot of extras, like rolls or cake or something special, and everything is excellent. I'm going to be spoiled by the time I leave." Robin paused. "I can't believe it's Wednesday already. We leave Sunday, and then I have to get back to real life."

"I'm glad you're having a good time," he said. "When we met on Monday, it seemed like you'd rather be anywhere but here."

She stared down at the picnic table, knowing she was blushing. "I guess I've gotten over myself a bit. You don't know how nice it is to talk to someone with no expectations. No history. Just a friend."

"I do." Rick smiled, and those little crinkles appeared at the corners of his eyes.

Robin had to admit that Rick was handsome, but she reminded herself that he was married and pushed away the soft tug of attraction she felt.

"Can we play in the water now?" Katie asked, shoving her empty plate aside. "We're done."

"Please?" Will added.

"Okay, but stay close, and don't go into the water past your knees," Rick answered. "We'll have to leave before long."

Katie and Will raced to the lake and began splashing around. The sun, high above their heads, was warm enough to make it a pleasant day.

He smiled as he watched the children. "I don't know what I ever did without them."

"You're a good dad. Some guys aren't very involved with raising their kids. I'm sure your wife appreciates all you do," Robin said, wondering if Rick would introduce her to his wife when she returned from lunch. Rick was kind, and Robin assumed his wife was too. She was obviously not the outdoorsy type because Robin had never seen her outside with him and the kids.

Rick ran one hand through the dark curls at the back of his neck. "Yeah, well, my wife—"

There was a sudden shriek from the lakeshore.

"Daddy!" Katie cried as she threw her arm around her wailing brother.

Robin and Rick jumped to their feet and ran to them.

"What happened?" Rick asked, taking Will into his arms. "What's wrong?"

"It hurts." Will sobbed, holding out his bleeding left foot. "It hurts bad."

"Don't worry," Rick soothed, bracing the boy against him as he inspected the cut. "It'll be all right. We'll get it fixed up. Come on." He took Will in his arms and carried him back toward the picnic table.

Robin ran ahead of Rick, grabbed all the paper napkins they had brought, and handed the wad to him. Will had bled down the right leg of Rick's pants, and the napkins were quickly soaked.

"I'd better get a towel or something," Rick said to Robin. "Can you stay with them a minute?"

Will clung to his neck. "No, Daddy, don't go."

Katie was hanging on Rick's arm, anxiously watching her brother.

"I can get something if you want," Robin offered.

Rick fished in his pocket for his room key and passed it to Robin. "The room number is on there. If you wouldn't mind, please get a couple of towels out of the bathroom. Then I can take Will to the ER and have them examine the cut. It looks like he stepped on a piece of glass."

Robin hurried to The Tidewater and found their room. She knocked in case Rick's wife had come back from lunch.

When there was no answer, she unlocked the door and walked inside. The room had already been tidied for the day, the two queen beds had been made up, the bathroom cleaned. A woman's toiletries were on one side of the counter, a man's on the other. She had known already it would be like that, but seeing it somehow gave her a twinge of disappointment.

Robin pushed away her ridiculous thoughts and grabbed two

fluffy white towels. She locked the door behind her and rushed to the picnic area.

As soon as she reached the family, she handed the towels and the key to Rick. "What else can I do?"

"Nothing now. But thanks." Rick took the sodden paper napkins away from Will's foot and replaced them with one of the towels, pressing hard. "Please don't hang on to me, honey," he said, easing his arm out of his daughter's grasp. "I need to get this to stop bleeding as much as I can."

Katie stepped back, tearful.

Robin pulled the obviously frightened girl close. "Will is going to be fine. Your daddy knows what to do."

Katie hid her face against Robin's side, peeping out just enough to watch what was happening with her brother.

Robin was touched that the little girl felt comfortable enough to use her as a source of comfort.

"I won't be able to hold the towel while I drive," Rick said, still keeping pressure on the cut. "I hate to ask you this, but do you think you could come with us?"

"I don't mind at all," Robin replied. She squeezed Katie's hand. "You can help me take care of Will. How's that?"

Katie nodded as she carefully patted her brother's leg above the makeshift swaddling. "You'll be okay. We're going to take care of you."

Rick gave Robin a grateful smile as he carried Will to a late-model sedan. "If you'll sit in the back, I can lay him next to you, and you can keep pressure on the cut."

"Got it." Robin slid into the back seat.

Rick settled Will into the car and placed his son's foot in Robin's lap. "Come on, Katie," he said. "You sit in the front with me. Remember that hospital sign we saw on the way here?"

She nodded.

"You can watch for the sign and help me find the hospital," Rick said, getting behind the wheel.

Katie agreed and hopped into the passenger seat.

As Rick drove to the hospital, he reassured Will that everything would be all right. Robin echoed his words and held Will's hand. The boy squeezed her hand in return. Katie kept glancing at her brother to see how he was doing.

"I almost forgot," Rick said. "I'd better let Mama know what happened." He made a brief call and promised to keep her updated.

When they arrived at the emergency room, Rick swiftly got out of the car, opened the back door, and picked up Will.

As they rushed to the door, Rick asked Robin, "Would you mind keeping an eye on Katie once I take him inside?" He looked down at his daughter. "It's probably not a good idea for everybody to be in there."

"Sure," Robin said. "Katie and I will be in the waiting room."

"We'll be right here, Will," Katie called as Rick carried the boy to the desk.

A moment later, Rick and Will disappeared through a set of double doors, leaving Robin and Katie to wait.

"He's going to be fine," Robin told Katie as they sat down on one of the vinyl-covered sofas in the lounge.

Katie frowned. "People shouldn't leave glass where other people are walking barefoot."

"You're right," Robin said. "They ought to pick up after themselves."

"Will is only a baby," Katie said, curling up against Robin's side. "But don't tell him, because it makes him mad."

"It'll be our secret," Robin promised.

As they waited, Robin flipped through a magazine without really seeing it, and Katie did the same with a children's book from a small bookshelf in the corner. The minutes seemed to pass slowly.

By the time Rick entered the waiting room with Will, Robin had perused three magazines and Katie was fast asleep.

"Will and your daddy are here," Robin said, gently jostling the girl's shoulder. "It's time to go."

"Will is as good as new," Rick announced. He shifted his son to his hip and reached down for Katie's hand. "Come on."

Katie blinked at her brother's bandaged foot. "That doesn't look so bad."

"I was brave," Will said, despite the quaver in his voice.

"Yes, you were," Rick said.

"I can tell you were." Robin reached over to push a wisp of dark hair off the boy's forehead. "I'm very proud of you."

Will ducked his head against his father's neck.

They walked out of the hospital and to the car.

"Thanks for helping out," Rick said once they got the kids buckled into the back seat. Then he set one of the hospital's plastic bags on the floorboard. "Now to see if I can get those towels decently clean before the staff at the inn finds them." He opened the front passenger door for Robin.

"They probably know how to deal with it themselves," she said as she got in. "I wouldn't worry about it."

He shrugged. "Cold water usually works if you rinse something enough times."

During the ride to the inn, Will went into great detail about his visit to the hospital, telling his sister everything the doctors had done.

Rick glanced at Robin. "He's making most of that up," he muttered under his breath. "They didn't let him see while they were cleaning out the wound and putting in the stitches. But he was very brave. I know he was scared."

"I'm sure it helped to have you there with him," Robin said.

"I wouldn't have had it any other way. I'm afraid I didn't have much of a dad myself, and I wasn't about to raise my kids—" He stopped abruptly, staring at the road ahead. "Sorry. I know we said we weren't going to talk about the past."

"It's all right," Robin said, meaning it. "I've been thinking about what you said to me."

"What was that?" Rick asked.

"You said to enjoy the here and now, and you were right. It's been refreshing hanging out with you and your kids. My mom means well, but I always feel like she's trying to push me into doing something fun. And I guess I've pushed back and held on to someone who's gone. I should have already let him go and dealt with his death. But coming here and getting away from my everyday life at home has made me feel a bit like I did when I was kid."

"I'm glad." Rick smiled at her warmly. "I understand about hanging on to grief too. It feels like you didn't care enough about the one you lost if you let go too soon, but that's not true. And the other person, if he loved you at all, wouldn't want you wasting your life wishing him back. I'll bet you anything that he would tell you to get out there and live."

Robin nodded. She could picture Jason saying that. She always thought of him as he had looked the last time she'd seen him. He'd been wearing jeans, an old T-shirt, and a beat-up baseball cap with his high school mascot on it. They'd been at a nursery shopping for trees—trees of all things—because the first thing he had wanted to do when they got married and bought a house was plant a big tree in the backyard.

"Something for the kids to play in when we have them," Jason had told her. "A place we can hang a good tire swing. I'm thinking oak."

He had inspected every oak tree that nursery had, including the scrawny small ones that probably wouldn't last through the winter.

It had never surprised Robin in the least to hear that Jason had gone into the floodwater to rescue a woman and her child. Robin also knew that he had done it not only to try to save the two of them but because he loved the rush and the risk. Because he wanted to live while he was alive.

Maybe Jason had been too sure he was indestructible, and maybe she was still a little bit angry with him for not being more careful that day, but that had been part of what made him who he was. Robin knew that Jason never would have wanted her to bury herself alongside him. If it had been him, he wouldn't have hidden himself away, afraid to even peek out his door, and he definitely wouldn't want her to live that way.

A smile twitched at the corner of her mouth. How many times had her mother said the same thing? And now, from a near stranger, it finally made sense.

"What?" Rick asked her.

Her smile vanished.

"I'm right, aren't I? About whoever it was." He signaled as they approached the turn toward Lake Haven. "I'll drop you off. Your mom might be worried about you."

Robin checked her watch. "Yeah, I guess you'd better."

The chatter from the back seat abruptly stopped.

"Are you going to play with us again tomorrow, Miss Robin?" Katie asked.

"I can't swim anymore," Will grumbled. "Or go barefoot."

"Just for a while," Rick reminded him. "You want your foot to get better fast, right?"

"Yeah," Will admitted.

"Okay, then you need to do what the doctor told you," Rick said. "And you have to rest too. So maybe we'd better take it easy tomorrow."

Robin turned around in her seat to see two pouting faces. "I'll tell you what. Tomorrow I'll be drawing outside the inn where I'm staying. As long as you wear your shoes and don't get too tired, we could have another art lesson. How would that be?"

Katie's eyes lit up. "Can we?"

"I'll wear my shoes," Will promised. "Please, Daddy?"

Rick chuckled and glanced at Robin. "You don't have to keep my kids entertained if you don't want to."

"I'd enjoy it," Robin said. "Honestly, I haven't had this much fun since—well, in a long time. What do you think? You don't have anything else planned, do you?"

"Not in the morning," Rick answered. "We promised Mama we'd all go out to the antique place in the afternoon, but she won't mind if the kids come see you first."

"What do you think?" Robin asked Katie and Will.

"Yes, please," Katie said.

"Can you teach us to draw doctors and nurses?" Will asked.

"We'll see what we can come up with," Robin answered.

They arrived at the Magnolia Harbor Inn, and Rick stopped the car. "Thanks again for all your help. And for the art lessons."

"It's my pleasure," Robin said. "See you tomorrow." She got out of the car and waved at the kids.

She wasn't surprised to see her mother waiting for her when she walked into the inn.

"I saw you pull up," Mom said. "Is everything all right?"

"Will stepped on a piece of glass, and we took him to the ER to get stitched up," Robin said. "But he's fine now."

"I'm glad it's nothing serious," Mom said, examining her as only a mother could. "You look like you've been having a good time."

A snarky response immediately leaped to Robin's tongue, but she smiled instead. "Yeah, I have."

The concern in her mother's eyes increased rather than lessened. "Honey . . ."

"What? I thought you wanted me to come here and enjoy myself."

"I did." Mom reached over and tucked a wisp of hair behind Robin's ear. "I do. I do very much."

"But?"

"You seem to like Katie and Will a lot."

Robin nodded. "So?"

"You seem to like their dad a lot too," Mom said.

Robin rolled her eyes. "I realize he's married, okay? I'm not going after him or anything."

"I'm not saying that. I know you wouldn't mean to fall in love with someone who's already married. From what you've told me, he seems like a perfect gentleman and a really nice guy." Her mother paused. "But I don't want you to get too attached."

"How can I get too attached?" Robin protested. "I've mostly played with the kids. I've only spoken to him briefly, and I told him that I don't want to talk about anything in the past. Besides, he hasn't shown any romantic interest in me."

Robin hesitated. It was true that Rick hadn't made any moves, but maybe there had been a moment or two when she wished he would. She hadn't felt so comfortable and happy with anyone since Jason. Then again, she hadn't allowed herself to relax around anyone since Jason.

"Anyway, we're leaving Sunday," Robin concluded. "How attached can anybody be by then?"

Mom nodded, although she didn't seem reassured. "Just be careful. Perhaps it's not a good idea for you to spend every day with them."

"Not every day," she corrected. "I promised to give the kids another art lesson tomorrow morning, but that's all. I'm going to the book fair on Friday by myself."

"As much as I would love for you to meet someone new, I don't want you to get hurt over someone who could never be right for you," her mom persisted.

"I'll be careful." Robin leaned over and kissed her mother's cheek. "Thanks for letting me come here with you. I'm going to our room." When she got halfway up the stairs, she turned to see her mother staring after her. "I'll be down for dinner."

Winston bounded into the room from somewhere in the back of the inn and raced up the stairs to her.

"I missed you too," Robin said, catching the dog in her arms and kissing his sweet face. Avoiding the knowing look in her mother's eyes, she spun around and hurried up to their suite.

14

Brenda

Jessica finished putting on her makeup and then stowed her suitcase under her rollaway bed. "I'm going down to breakfast. You two had better hurry." With a smile and a wave, she was gone.

Brenda stood in front of the bathroom mirror, an old plastic headband pushing her hair away from her makeup-free face. She had let Tess and Jessica and the three women in the connecting Bluebell Suite use the bathroom first. They were all eager to go to breakfast so they could resume their sewing. But the thought of going downstairs and seeing Libby made Brenda feel a bit queasy.

Tess poked her head into the bathroom. "Are you coming?"

"You go ahead," Brenda answered. "I'll be there in a minute."

Tess didn't move until Brenda met her eyes in the mirror. "Will you really?"

Brenda stared down at the sink. "I don't know."

Tess went over to Brenda and put one arm around her. "Are you all right?"

"Why does this hurt so much right now?" Brenda asked, her throat tightening around the words. "Libby and I haven't talked in three years. It's how things are. I need to accept it."

"I know how much you wanted this to work out," Tess said. "Of course it hurts when it hasn't yet."

"It's never going to happen!" Brenda snapped. She swallowed hard and reached up to clasp Tess's hand on her shoulder. "I'm sorry. I know you're trying to help, but I'm afraid this is only making things worse between Libby and me. I shouldn't have tried it in the first place."

"I realize this hasn't been easy for you," Tess said. "Libby can be intimidating, and I don't want you to feel like you have to do something you'd rather not."

Brenda turned to face her friend. "I've greatly appreciated your being here for me, especially around Libby. And maybe I needed somebody to push me out of my comfort zone. But I doubt it's doing any good."

"There's no guarantee that Libby will ever change her mind," Tess said, sympathy and understanding in her expression. "I wish I could promise you something different."

"So should I keep trying or not?" Brenda asked.

Tess shook her head and chuckled. "Oh no. I'm not going to make that decision for you."

"What would you do?" Brenda pressed.

"I'm not sure," Tess replied. "I suppose I'd ask myself if I would be sorry I hadn't tried my best."

Brenda nodded.

"Come downstairs when you're ready," Tess said as she gave her a hug. "Don't forget we have that strip-piecing demo later, if you're interested."

"I don't know what I'm going to do," Brenda admitted.

"What should I say when someone asks about you?"

"Tell them I'll catch up."

"Let me know if you want company," Tess offered. "Can I bring you some breakfast?"

"No thanks," Brenda said. "You go ahead."

She was glad when Tess left her alone. However, Brenda was immediately sorry that she hadn't accepted Tess's offer of food. She wasn't actually hungry, but she should eat something. Maybe Grace or Charlotte would be willing to send something up. Then she could skip lunch, eat a bite of dinner tonight, and feel stronger tomorrow. This would be over Sunday, and she could go back to having Libby pretend she didn't exist.

Brenda decided to read the novel she'd brought with her. The Regency romance was light and witty, and it was just the thing to cheer her up and make the day pass quickly.

When she opened her suitcase to retrieve the book, she saw her photo album. She put her hand on it, meaning to push it aside and get the book underneath it, but she picked it up instead and carried it to the damask armchair that had been crammed into the corner to make room for Jessica's rollaway bed.

She flipped through the pages again. Birthdays and Christmases. Joys and sorrows. Successes and failures. Friends and family, mostly gone. Who was she kidding? They were all gone. Brenda only had Libby. Libby only had her. Except they didn't. And they wouldn't if neither of them tried to fix the rift between them.

But they would never reconcile if both of them weren't willing to try. Brenda couldn't do it all by herself. She had always heard that two couldn't walk together unless they agreed. Brenda and Libby didn't have to agree on everything, but they did have to agree to at least talk things out. There couldn't be any kind of relationship without that.

Closing her eyes, Brenda let her chin sink to her chest. What was she supposed to do? She didn't want to hang on to the hurt, anger, and bitterness that she carried because she knew how corrosive those emotions were. She didn't expect to be Libby's best friend before everyone left the inn. Brenda simply wanted to try to work things out, and she wanted Libby to try too.

What was she willing to do to get Libby to hear her out? Give her the sewing machine? If Brenda thought that would solve the problem, she would do it. She almost had, but Grace had been right. This wasn't really about a sewing machine. Brenda could let Libby bully her into doing what she wanted all the time, or she could walk away and lose her forever. What kind of choice was that? What should she do? What could she do? After so long, why was it so important right now to do something?

Tears slipped from the corners of her eyes, and she prayed, *God, help me. Please show me what to do.*

There was only silence in the room, silence and the rhythmic *tick, tick, tick* of the travel alarm clock Tess had left on the nightstand.

Brenda glanced down at the album in her lap. Her hand was covering one of the pictures, and she moved it a few inches away.

She remembered that day like it was yesterday. When Brenda arrived at Grandma's house that summer to stay, Libby had surprised Brenda with a dress made of soft yellow chiffon that was pretty enough to be worn to church. Libby had been so excited to give it to her. Brenda could still hear the delight in Grandma's voice when she announced that Libby had made the dress by herself and that she had spent her own hard-earned pocket money on the material.

In the picture, Brenda was wearing that dress and gazing at her older cousin with adoration. Libby was gesturing dramatically toward her like a model on a game show. She used to smile a lot more when she was young. Behind them was Grandma, her expression warm and full of pride in her girls. She would be brokenhearted if she knew her granddaughters couldn't even speak civilly to each other. What would Grandma want Brenda to do now?

Brenda recalled the conversation she'd had with Grace and the advice she'd given her. *Be willing to talk to Libby if she wants to talk. Be kind. Have a good time with your friends no matter what she does. Don't let her get to you.*

Brenda could do that. She had been doing that. Everything but the last part . . .

Well, she could do that too, couldn't she? At the very least, she'd leave the Magnolia Harbor Inn knowing she had done everything she could to reach out to her cousin. That was why she'd come here. She couldn't let the opportunity pass her by. There may never be another one.

Brenda straightened her shoulders and walked over to the mirror once again. Then she checked her watch. She had just enough time to get herself fixed up and have breakfast before the strip-piecing class started.

15

Robin

The sunrise over Lake Haven was glorious to see. Robin sat on the veranda watching the dawn sky turn from deep purple to lavender and blue pierced by fingers of red and orange. The fluffy clouds were dark on the bottom, haloed with gold and white as the sun boiled over the horizon, turning the lake to fire and changing the stark black silhouettes of the trees to the softening greens and yellows of approaching autumn.

Normally, Robin wasn't a morning person. She tended to sleep in as late as possible, waiting till the last minute to get dressed and rush off to work. Once there, she lost herself in numbers and regulations, reassured by their changelessness and self-sufficiency. They tired only her mind and left her emotions comfortably tucked out of sight. Out of sight, out of mind.

But this morning she had been eager to start the day. Careful not to wake her mother, she had dressed quickly and slipped out of the suite, making her steps as light as possible as she went down the two flights of stairs.

Only Winston had been there to greet her, and he followed her out to the lake. Robin would have liked a cup of coffee to savor along with the new dawn, but she hadn't thought it very likely that even the hardworking sisters who owned the inn would be awake yet. She didn't need anything anyway. The quiet of the morning was enough for now. Enough to let her think.

It seemed strange to think ahead and not back, but it was a nice kind of strange, the kind she mulled over in her mind to make sure she liked it. It might take some getting used to, but maybe that would be fun too.

For the moment, Robin looked forward to giving Katie and Will another art lesson and simply enjoying herself. She knew she would miss the kids and Rick when she left Magnolia Harbor, but perhaps this brief time was all she needed with them. They had helped her realize that there were still interesting things to see and do and many kind people to meet. All she had to do was give it a try.

That was exactly what her mother had been trying to tell her. Robin realized she had ignored her mom for too long.

As the sun rose higher in the sky, the shadows of the trees became shorter. Mom would be wondering where she was by now. If Robin was going to have breakfast with the other women this morning, it would be a good idea to shower and put on clean clothes. She was ready for that cup of coffee too.

Robin and Winston went up to the Wisteria Loft Suite and found her mother already showered and dressed.

"I was going to check if my car was still outside," Mom teased. "I thought maybe you'd decided to take off on me."

Robin rolled her eyes good-naturedly. "Yeah, like I was going to abandon you without a word. I just felt like getting out early this morning."

"That sounds lovely." Mom gave her a quick hug. "I was about to go to breakfast. I don't know what the ladies have made for us this morning, but judging by what they've served us so far, I don't want to miss it. Are you coming?"

"I didn't realize how long I sat out there," Robin said. "I need to shower and get ready before any real people see me."

"So they're real people." Mom put her hands on her hips. "And what does that make me?"

Robin laughed. "Go ahead. Your friends will be waiting for you. I'll be down in a minute."

"That's all right. Take your time. I'll wait right here with Winston." Mom squeezed her hand. "It would be nice to have breakfast together."

"I'll hurry," Robin said. She grabbed her things and headed to the bathroom.

They made it downstairs a few minutes after the rest of the quilters had taken their seats on the veranda. Robin and her mother filled their plates with scrambled eggs, toast, and bacon.

Wanda waved them over, and they sat across from her.

Robin gazed at the lake, then checked her watch. Rick and the kids wouldn't be by for at least another hour. Maybe longer.

"Waiting for something?" Wanda asked.

Robin flushed and fumbled with her forkful of scrambled eggs. Still, she smiled. "Just expecting some friends later."

"Good for you," Wanda said. "Spending time with friends is more enjoyable than sitting out here by yourself."

"I haven't been by myself all that much," Robin told her. "And it is enjoyable."

"You can always learn how to quilt," Wanda said, smiling. "We're having another demonstration later this morning. You're more than welcome to join us."

Robin wasn't sure if she wanted to accept the invitation, but she thought it would be rude to say no to Wanda. "Maybe I will."

Her mom raised her eyebrows.

"I'd like to talk to you about a new quilt I want to design," Wanda continued. "Some people think the color combinations are too wild, but I like them. Since you're an artist, maybe you can tell me if one of the color theories fits what I want to do." Wanda grinned at Robin's mother. "Not that I don't know my own mind about what I want to make."

"You've got that right," Mom chimed in.

The older women chuckled.

"Would you mind checking out my fabrics and giving me your opinion?" Wanda asked Robin.

"I'd be happy to," Robin said, suddenly intrigued by Wanda's project. She decided to attend the session too. Maybe it was time for her to take a chance on something new. "And I'll stop by the demonstration and see why everyone is so crazy about quilting. Mom's been trying to get me interested for years."

"For all the good it's done me," Mom said, taking a demure sip of her coffee.

Wanda leaned a little closer to Robin. "Once you give it a try, you'll never go back."

"We'll see," Robin said.

Several of the other women made encouraging remarks. They were clearly pleased that Robin had agreed to join them for the demonstration. The twins, Amanda and Kathleen, started talking about when they did their first quilts.

Robin bit into a piece of perfectly prepared wheat toast, enjoying the chatter, wondering if she might like quilting after all, and then she noticed her mother observing her.

Mom quickly turned her attention to her breakfast.

But Robin had already read her mother's expression. She knew her mom was thinking of their conversation the night before and she was worried. Well, she didn't have to be.

Robin took another bite of toast, smiling at her mother as she chewed. She could enjoy spending time with Rick and the kids, and it didn't have to mean anything.

After breakfast, Robin went up to the loft and retrieved her sketch pads and pencils. Then she descended the stairs, left the inn, and strolled to the lake.

She sat on the grass and sketched out simple drawings of doctors and nurses. While she worked, she started to have fun imagining not only people in doctors' coats and nurses' uniforms but various dogs, cats, farm animals, and even sea creatures. Will had certainly requested an interesting subject matter.

Robin grinned as she drew a crab doctor using his claw to cut the thread on his dolphin patient's fin. The kids would get a kick out of that one. She was adding a whale nurse and a pelican holding an IV bag when she heard footsteps approaching.

Rick waved when he saw her waiting for them. "Good morning."

"Miss Robin!"

Both children ran to her, though Will was slower and more cautious than his big sister.

"Daddy said we couldn't come if I wasn't careful," he said once he reached her.

"Then you'd better be careful," she said, tapping his nose with one finger and then hugging him close.

"Where's Winston?" he asked. "Isn't he coming?"

"I don't know," Robin said. "He was taking a nap when I saw him last, but he'll probably be around sooner or later."

"Are we going to draw again?" Katie asked as she hugged Robin. "Can we draw fishes?"

"Sure, but I thought you wanted to draw doctors and nurses," Robin said. "I sketched some for you." She showed them the pictures she had done.

The kids giggled appreciatively.

"He's sewing up that dolphin," Will said, poking the drawing with one finger. "That's like when I was at the hospital."

Rick chuckled. "That's not bad. You ought to do children's books or something."

Robin stared at her hands. "I don't have that kind of training."

"You never know unless you try," Rick said.

Robin wasn't sure how to respond, so she focused on the children instead. "Are we ready to do some more drawing? Are we going to try doctors and nurses?"

"I want to draw fishes," Katie said. "Will wanted to draw doctors and nurses."

"I want to draw robots," Will insisted. "Can we draw robots?"

"Okay," Robin said, handing them sketch pads and pencils. "Robots and fishes. Let's see."

Rick smiled at Robin as she sketched out a few new ideas. She hadn't exactly been prepared for fish and robots, and she definitely hadn't been ready for the warmth that came into her face when Rick smiled at her.

"Now, let's see what you can do," she told the children once she had finished her examples. "Just remember what I told you."

Katie and Will sat cross-legged under the large magnolia tree that shaded the area and went to work on their pictures.

Rick sat down on the grass next to Robin. "I think you should do something with your art. You're very talented."

"Thanks." She started embellishing the simple fish she had drawn for Katie, adding scales and shading, gills, and even some eyelashes. "I have a boring but steady job, and I like it that way."

He cocked his head. "Do you really?"

For a moment, Robin met his gaze defiantly. Then she laughed. "Well, maybe not so much. But I have to earn a living somehow."

"Of course you do." Rick motioned to her drawing. "But you've heard people say that if you find something to do that you love, then you'll never work a day in your life."

"It's not finding work you like that's hard," she said. "It's getting someone to pay you for it on a regular basis."

"I guess that's true, but it wouldn't hurt to look into it, would it?" Rick asked. "I mean, if that kind of thing interests you."

Robin had never seriously considered becoming a real artist before. Sure, she had always fantasized about it, but it wasn't a practical career. She had gotten her degree in business administration with an emphasis in accounting because she knew she could always find a job with those credentials. Only a few artists actually made a living at it, right? The rest were waiters and greeters or took tickets at the local theater or scooped ice cream.

She didn't say any of that to Rick. It sounded too cynical, and what did she truly know about it? She had never attempted to do anything commercial with her drawing. But she had to admit that somehow Rick was making her want to give it a try.

"Maybe I'll check into it sometime," Robin finally conceded. "It might be interesting."

He nodded, appearing pleased. "I know a couple of test critics you could run your ideas past. They wouldn't be a scientific survey or anything, but they'd certainly let you know if they liked something."

Robin regarded her sketch of the sea creatures in the hospital. It might make a cute story. "I'll have to think about it." But she didn't know how the kids would be able to give their opinion on her work if they never saw her again after Sunday. The thought of that put a little lump in her throat.

Pushing away those thoughts, Robin reminded herself to enjoy the day and her remaining time at the inn. When the week was over, she'd return to her real life. She pressed her lips into a hard line. And Rick would return to his. Wife and all.

She spent the rest of the morning talking to Rick and helping the children with their drawings.

And when it was time for them to leave, she let them go.

16

Debbie

Debbie held out for as long as she could. When she couldn't take it anymore, she retrieved a stolen pill and swallowed it, chasing it down with water from the bathroom tap. Then she leaned against the countertop, soothed by the coolness of the granite and the quiet of the empty suite.

She wanted to keep hiding out in her room, but she'd have to rejoin the other ladies soon. One of the women from Winnie's quilting group was supposed to give them tips on strip piecing. What else could there possibly be to learn about it? Everyone had been sewing that way for years. Still, the sample was very interesting. It featured beautiful pieced stars that were supposedly much easier to make than they appeared.

Debbie didn't want to attend the session. She knew she wouldn't be able to concentrate on learning something new. But if she didn't go and smile and chatter, they'd know. Everyone would know.

She managed to straighten up. She had taken what she needed. She could do this. All she had to do was smile.

When Debbie walked into the dining room, she was surprised to see Winnie there waiting for her.

"I saved you a place," Winnie said, patting the chair next to her.

Debbie glanced over at Libby. No doubt Libby was expecting her to sit at her table, but Libby was searching for something in her sewing box and hadn't noticed her come in. She slipped into the seat next to Winnie. "I didn't know you were going to attend the class."

"I'm curious about Judith's star method," Winnie said. "She's been telling The Busy Bees about it for a while now, and she's never gotten around to showing us. I can't wait to see how she makes stars with all those little pieces. She says it wastes a lot of fabric doing it her way, but I wouldn't mind if I could get my piecing to turn out so perfectly."

"Your piecing is always gorgeous," Debbie said, though she was wondering how long this demonstration would last and when she could excuse herself for a while. That granite countertop in the bathroom had felt so nice and cool . . .

"Debbie?"

She blinked, realizing that Winnie had been talking to her. Or had the class started?

"Is everything all right?" Winnie asked. She sounded concerned.

Debbie smiled. "Of course. I was just thinking about the log cabin quilt I'm working on. Did I show it to you? I can't decide which of my border fabrics would look best with it. Libby says the purple, but she always picks purple."

Winnie watched her without commenting.

"What is it?" Debbie asked. She wasn't feeling very well, but she didn't think it showed in her face.

"Are you sure you're okay?" Winnie asked, pressing one hand to her arm. "You feel a little bit warm."

It was true Debbie felt warm, but she didn't know it was obvious. She swiped one hand across her upper lip, relieved that she wasn't sweating. Again, she smiled. "It's nothing."

Winnie didn't seem convinced, but she didn't press the matter.

Before Debbie could change the subject, a woman in her late fifties entered the room. "Good afternoon, ladies."

The assembled group greeted her.

"I'm Judith Mason from The Busy Bees, and I own Spool & Thread, a fabric shop located in downtown Magnolia Harbor. I'm delighted to be here to talk about strip piecing."

The door opened, and Robin tentatively stepped inside the room. "Sorry I'm late. I didn't mean to interrupt."

Judith smiled. "We're just getting started. Please come in and join us."

"There's an empty chair next to me," Wanda piped up.

Robin thanked the older woman as she took the seat next to her.

"Now here's one of my pieced stars." Judith displayed the example and began explaining her method.

Debbie wasn't sure if the demonstration lasted thirty minutes or three hours. Her seams weren't straight and her points didn't match, but somehow she stumbled through the steps Judith showed them. And if her block resembled a snowball instead of a star, nobody mentioned it.

The minute Judith was finished, Debbie stood up and excused herself.

Again, Winnie stared at her strangely. "Are you sure you're all right?"

"I just need the ladies' room," Debbie said. She was out of the room and up the stairs before she realized Winnie was right behind her. She stopped at the door to her suite.

"There's a public restroom downstairs," Winnie reminded her.

"I, uh, need to get my medication in my room. I forgot to take it earlier." Debbie laughed thinly. "Maybe that's why I've been feeling so odd."

Winnie didn't respond as she remained standing there.

"I'll see you downstairs in a minute," Debbie said, trying again to get her friend to leave.

Winnie put one hand on Debbie's arm. "Will you talk to me for a minute?"

"Well, I need to take my medication, but I'll come back downstairs as quick as I can. Wasn't the class great? I love those stars Judith showed us. I was thinking I could put them in a quilt and make it red, white, and blue—"

"Please, Debbie, can we talk?"

"We have those stockings to make for the retirement home," Debbie babbled on, avoiding Winnie's question. "After that we're supposed to plan for the next raffle quilt. And tonight—"

"Please," Winnie insisted.

Biting her lip, Debbie opened the door and let her friend into the room. Maybe Winnie wanted to talk about something else. Perhaps she was searching for volunteers for a charity project. Or maybe Winnie had a personal problem she wanted to discuss with her. Debbie's stomach knotted as she shut the door behind her. No, it was nothing like that.

Winnie sat in one of the overstuffed chairs in front of the fireplace and invited Debbie to take the other one.

Debbie perched on the edge of the chair, her hands clasped in her lap.

Winnie reached over to unclasp them. "I just want to talk," she said gently. "This isn't an interrogation."

Debbie laughed, though it wasn't a very convincing laugh. "Don't be silly. Now what did you want to talk about?"

"I wanted you to know that if you ever need anything, I'll be happy to help."

"I know that already," Debbie assured her. "We've been friends too long for me to think anything else."

"But we haven't spent much time together in quite a while," Winnie said. "I'm wondering if everything's okay."

Debbie tried to act puzzled and slightly amused. "You know how it is with me. There's nothing much going on. It's always the same old routine day in, day out."

Winnie's expression was grave. "I'm having trouble believing that right now. I can tell something's wrong. Please talk to me. I'm not trying to embarrass you or make you feel bad. I want to be your friend. Isn't there any way I can help you?"

Debbie smiled at her, but then her eyes filled with tears. "You won't want to be my friend if you knew what a mess I'm in."

"There's nothing in the world that would make me feel that way," Winnie said gently. "Tell me what's going on."

Sighing, Debbie pushed her glasses up on her head, then took them off entirely so she could scrub her eyes with the heels of her hands. "I didn't mean for this to happen. I didn't think it could happen. Not to me."

"Of course you didn't," Winnie said.

Debbie patted her shirt pocket for the little wad of tissues she had used earlier that day. "You know I had surgery on my back about a year ago."

Winnie nodded. "Has it been bothering you? I understand there are many good pain medications you could talk to your doctor about—"

"I know all about those," Debbie interrupted, dabbing at her eyes. "They work. Maybe they work too well."

"What do you mean?"

Debbie dropped her head. "I don't want you to hate me."

"Hate you?" Winnie asked, obviously surprised. "I could never do that. What's wrong?"

"I've been having trouble with those pills." Debbie took a shaky breath. "I can't stop taking them. I understand they're not good for me, especially since I don't need them for pain, but it's so hard."

"I've heard about that," Winnie said. "When people start taking certain pain pills, it's easy for them to become dependent on them, but they don't mean to get addicted."

"I've been so afraid that someone might find out." Debbie grabbed Winnie's hand. "You won't tell anybody about this, will you?"

Winnie shook her head. "I only want to help you. I want you to be all right. I could tell you haven't been feeling well."

"I'm so ashamed. How could I have let myself become an . . . ?" Debbie didn't say the word *addict*. An addict was someone who lived on the street and ate out of trash cans, somebody who robbed pharmacies and sold drugs to kids to support a ferocious habit. She didn't say anything about the pills she had stolen from her friends. She didn't have to tell Winnie about that.

"It happens to many people," Winnie said. "It's not your fault. But there are things you can do to get assistance. Have you talked to your doctor about it?"

"Not yet. I don't want him to stop seeing me." And Debbie didn't want him to stop filling her prescriptions.

"Helping you with this kind of problem is his job," Winnie reminded her.

"I know. But some of my friends see him too. I wouldn't want any of them finding out about this. I don't want anyone to know." Debbie took hold of Winnie's sleeve. "Please don't say anything."

"I promise I won't. But what about seeing someone else, someone who specializes in addictions? Even a clinic might help you. A place like that would have counselors and everything."

"It's fine." Debbie blew her nose and smiled. "I've been having a bad day, but I'm dealing with it. Once I make up my mind to do something, that's all it takes. I guess this wasn't the best time to quit, but there's no time like the present, right?"

Winnie didn't believe her. Debbie could see it in her eyes, in the wary tautness of her mouth.

Debbie was going to quit, but she couldn't do it at the moment.

There was too much she had to do during the retreat—projects to coordinate for the group, meals to prepare and serve, and of course there was Libby to keep placated. If Brenda wanted to make up with Libby, she was going about it all wrong. Letting Libby have her own way always made things easier, and what did it hurt? But when things were going a little more smoothly, Debbie would quit. She could do it then.

"I'm glad you're trying to stop," Winnie said, "but it must be hard to do on your own. You should get professional help."

"I know, but I can do it," Debbie told her. Maybe it hadn't been a good idea to let Winnie know what she was struggling with, but there was no need to let her think she couldn't handle it. "It eventually comes down to being able to handle it on my own anyway, doesn't it? I mean, a counselor or a doctor can't be with me every minute."

"That's true," Winnie admitted.

Debbie exhaled and settled her glasses back into place. "I'm sorry to have made this sound like such a major problem. I've been having a rough time this week, but that's pretty much to be expected during the retreat. It's nice to tell somebody about it, but there's no need for you to worry. Once I get through this rough patch, I'll be completely fine."

Winnie nodded, still not looking convinced, and stood up. "So how are you feeling? Better?"

"Yes." Debbie did feel slightly better after opening up to her friend. If only she could stay in her room and rest for a while.

"Are you going to have lunch with the group?" Winnie asked.

"Oh, sure." Debbie checked her watch. "It's nearly time, isn't it? Let me stop in the bathroom for a minute, and we can go down and see what needs to be done in the kitchen."

Before Winnie could protest or ask any more questions, Debbie went into the bathroom and shut the door. She had to keep going. Somehow she had to get through this retreat. She swallowed another pill. Then she removed her glasses and splashed cold water on her face. That was better. Now she could make it through lunch and the rest of the afternoon.

Debbie reached into her pocket for her lipstick and felt the folded piece of paper she had put there earlier in the day. She needed to throw it away or flush it down the toilet so nobody accidentally found it and read it. Besides, it wasn't going to help anything. Why in the world had she written it in the first place?

It was because of the hatbox at the reception desk. The box allowed her to tell the truth about herself. It didn't judge or scold, and it assured her that she wasn't alone.

Debbie unfolded the paper carefully, trying to keep it from crackling. She didn't need Winnie hearing the sound and wondering what she was doing. The writing was uneven, slanting down the paper, the letters cramped and small, blurred together.

> *I can't tell my friends that I'm an addict and a thief. I don't know which one of those is worse. Or maybe the worst part is knowing what a horrible, weak person I am. I've tried to quit again and again. But no matter what I do, I can't stop taking pills I shouldn't need and stealing pills I shouldn't have.*
>
> *My friends wouldn't understand what it's like. They wouldn't want to be around me anymore. I have to just—*

She had broken off there because she had been interrupted. Libby had come out of the bathroom, so Debbie had stuffed the note and her pen into her pocket before Libby could ask her what she was writing.

Debbie scanned the pitiful scrap of paper again. Then she fished the pen out of her pocket and wrote one more line.

Please pray for me.

She folded the paper, hiding it and the pen in her pocket again. Then she forced a smile and opened the bathroom door. "Sorry to keep you waiting. Are you ready for lunch? I think we're having Ellen's Mexican casserole today."

"Are you sure it's okay if I join you?" Winnie asked. "I'm not actually part of the retreat."

"Of course it's okay," Debbie replied. "We always end up with more than we can eat, and you and your group have been so nice about having classes for us. Your friend Judith will be eating with us too."

"It does sound good," Winnie said, her concerned expression finally easing.

They didn't say anything as they descended the stairs.

When they reached the first floor, Debbie glanced at the dining room door. "Oh, I think I left my sewing machine light on."

"That's all right," Winnie said. "It won't use much electricity."

"No, it's one of those little battery-powered ones that you stick to the side of your machine so it'll shine right on your needle. If I leave it on too long, the battery will run out, and I won't be able to see a thing when I'm sewing. You know how blind I am."

"Okay, I'll wait for you."

"No, go ahead." Debbie nudged her friend toward the veranda.

Winnie seemed uneasy, but she didn't argue. "Don't be long."

"I'll be right there," Debbie promised, then headed toward the dining room. As soon as Winnie was out of sight, she detoured over to the hatbox perched on the corner of the reception desk.

Before she could lose her nerve, she slipped the lid off the box, dropped the paper from her pocket inside, and closed the box again. She needed to tell someone—anyone—what she was really going through.

She wasn't sure who would read her note. Winnie admitted that she sometimes read and responded to the letters, but Winnie already knew about Debbie's problem. Debbie was sure that Winnie hadn't believed her story about quitting, so if she read this note, it wouldn't matter. Perhaps Grace or Charlotte would read it. Whoever it was, Debbie needed someone to know.

"Please pray for me," she whispered.

Brenda

At dinner Thursday evening, Brenda counted down the days until they all left the inn Sunday afternoon. She couldn't wait for the whole ordeal to be over and done with.

Brenda had spent the day pretending to have a great time. She had sewn and chatted and eaten more than she would have at home. After the healthy portion of Mexican casserole she had consumed at lunch, she didn't feel like eating dinner. But she ate Frankie's chicken lasagna anyway. She couldn't let Libby see her not enjoying herself.

Sitting next to Brenda were Tess and Robin. Brenda had been surprised when Robin joined them for dinner, and she tried to make the younger woman feel welcome. But Robin focused on the food in front of her, and Brenda thought she seemed more preoccupied than usual.

Brenda couldn't help but glance at the other side of the table. Debbie sat beside Libby, smiling absently as Libby told the women around her how much everyone at her local sewing shop admired her quilts.

When Brenda glanced at Tess, she noticed a touch of amusement in her friend's eyes as she listened to Libby. Brenda allowed herself a hint of a smile in return.

"Is there something funny over there?" Libby demanded abruptly.

Brenda cringed inwardly. "Not funny, no, but kind of nice. I'm going to miss everyone when we go home on Sunday. It's been wonderful spending the days talking, sewing, and learning new techniques."

Okay, all of that was a total lie. The retreat had been nothing but stomach-roiling tension with Libby watching her every move. Still,

Brenda had managed to sound pleasant and unintimidated. At least that was something.

"Then again, it's not hard to feel good if you take enough pills, is it?" Libby said coolly.

Brenda's smile vanished. "What are you talking about?"

"I'm missing some painkillers," Libby said. "I guess I should have kept my suite locked up after all."

Tess stared at Libby, obviously startled. "You're missing pills too?"

"The other day I dropped a few aspirin down the bathroom sink," Debbie said. "How silly is that?"

"These weren't exactly aspirin," Libby said, giving Brenda a pointed look.

Brenda felt the blood drain from her face. "Are you accusing me of taking your pills?"

"I'd be willing to bet that you never told anybody about the little problem you had several years ago." Libby gazed down the length of the table like a presiding monarch. "It's an interesting story. Why don't you tell everybody about it?"

"I'm not sure what you mean," Brenda answered, narrowing her eyes.

"Go on," Libby said, her voice syrupy sweet. "If you've already told everybody everything about our family for the past fifty years, including how I ended up being raised by our grandmother, I don't see why you wouldn't be willing to talk about your surgery."

Brenda took a bite of lasagna, forcing herself to chew placidly. Most everybody here already knew she'd had back and neck surgery four years earlier. There wasn't anything shocking about that, so why was her pulse beating so hard and fast in her ears?

Libby glanced at the others around the table and made a slashing gesture across her throat. "They had to go through the front to get to her vertebrae."

"I know it sounds gruesome," Brenda responded, trying to keep her expression calm, "but it wasn't that bad. And the doctor was pretty good about making the cut where there was already a crease. Even I can hardly tell where the scar is unless I'm looking for it."

"My surgeon did that when I had my surgeries for carpal tunnel syndrome," Wanda chimed in. She displayed the underside of both of her wrists. "I guess that's one of the good things about being older. I had plenty of lines already. Who would notice a few more?"

Ellen shuddered, putting one elegantly manicured hand over her heart. "You were brave to have them both done at the same time. I don't think I could have managed."

"Well, I figured I'd miss the least amount of sewing time if I went ahead and did both," Wanda said with a grin. "It helped that my daughter was willing to wait on me hand and foot while I healed."

Several of the women began sharing their surgery stories. Libby's attempt to humiliate Brenda seemed to have already been forgotten by the others. Relieved, Brenda took another bite of her food.

Frankie launched into a long and often-told story about the time she had stepped wrong off her front porch and shattered her ankle. "It finally healed, but I had the hardest time. And those pain pills made me as sick as a dog."

"Some people take a real liking to painkillers and then can't give them up," Libby said, glancing at Brenda. "Even when they don't need them anymore."

Apparently, Libby hadn't given up trying to embarrass her. Brenda wanted to flee from the table and hide in her room. She turned to Tess for reassurance.

Tess gave her a calm smile. Tess was aware of what Brenda had been through after the surgery, and she knew how hard it had been.

Brenda took a deep breath. "It's a real problem. I had trouble getting off pain medication when I had my surgery, but it's been almost four years now since I even thought about taking pills."

Several of the ladies in the group smiled at her. They appeared understanding.

Debbie stared down at her barely touched plate and remained silent.

"That's easy enough to say." Libby eyed Brenda with disgust. "But that's how it is with addicts. They're too weak to keep off the medication, and then they lie about using it. When their doctors won't give them any more pills, they steal them from their friends and families." She raised her chin. "If they had any backbone, they'd just quit instead of sniveling about how hard it is. People like that make me sick."

Debbie was still staring at her plate. No doubt she was trying to figure out how to smooth over the squabble.

Brenda swallowed the tightness in her throat. She refused to let Libby make her cry. "I'm afraid it's not like that," she said, and she was amazed at the steady gravity in her voice.

"So, what is it like?" Libby challenged.

"Most people who get addicted to painkillers are desperate to quit taking them," Brenda said. "There are a lot of unpleasant physical, mental, financial, and social side effects. I was horrified to realize I was addicted. My addiction was pretty mild, and it still wasn't easy to quit. But I did quit. And I didn't steal any of your pills, Libby." She glanced at Tess. "Or yours."

"I know," Tess said simply.

"Of course you'd stand up for Brenda," Libby sneered at Tess. "I can't believe you don't care that she's robbing you blind in your own room."

"She is not stealing from me," Tess said firmly.

"Don't think your doctor will give you another prescription anytime soon," Libby continued. "My doctor is going to throw a fit when I ask him to give me more pills, but I don't mind telling him how my own cousin stole some from me."

"I didn't steal your pills!" Brenda burst out. She couldn't help the sudden tears that ran down her cheeks and her neck, leaving dark splotches on her denim shirt. "I haven't taken any prescription pain pills in nearly four years."

Carolyn got some tissues out of her purse and handed them to her. "Why don't we finish dinner? Then Libby and Brenda can talk about this in private."

"I hear relapses are pretty common," Libby went on, her expression smug and bland. "Some people realize there's an opportunity and don't have the spine to resist."

"And some people have an opportunity to run their mouths and don't have the decency to resist," Wanda retorted.

"How many pills are you missing?" Frankie asked, her eyes wide.

"Maybe you dropped a few without realizing it," Amanda suggested.

Her twin nodded. "Or didn't bring as many as you thought."

"I know exactly how many were in the bottle," Libby snapped. She glared at Brenda. "And I know exactly how many are missing. You can ask Debbie how careful I am with my medicine."

Everyone looked at Debbie, but she was still sitting there, not saying anything, not moving.

"I don't know anything about your medicine," Brenda said, "except that I didn't take any of it. And stop putting Debbie in the middle of things all the time. She hasn't done anything but try to keep the peace."

"It seems to me," Libby said, her voice getting lower as she obviously grew angrier, "that you're pretty nervous about Debbie saying anything about what she knows."

Brenda clenched her jaw, wishing she could scream. "I didn't—"

"Brenda wouldn't steal anything from anybody," Debbie interrupted, her chair legs scraping the floor as she stood. "I know she wouldn't, Libby. Please don't think she would. I know you're careful about your medicine, but perhaps you miscounted or something. Maybe they spilled out in your suitcase on the way here. Why don't you check and see?"

"Because I know," Libby stated, then studied Debbie. "You'd better sit down again before you fall on the floor."

"Are you sure you're all right, Debbie?" Carolyn asked.

Debbie braced herself against the table for a moment, and then she dredged up a wan smile. "I'm okay. I think I'll just go lie down for a while. This headache . . ." With an apologetic shrug, she hurried out of the room.

"So who's missing their painkillers besides me and Tess?" Libby asked once Debbie was gone. "I know we're not the only ones taking them."

"I think Carolyn's right," Tess said to Libby. "If you want to talk to your cousin about your medication, you can do it in private. Or we can all talk about it, but let's wait until after we've eaten. No use spoiling a delicious dinner, is there?"

"I thought everyone would like to know what's going on," Libby huffed. "From now on, I'm keeping my pills in my purse."

"Good for you," Tess said. "Now, let's talk about something more pleasant. Robin is going to think we're a bunch of squabbling old hens and never want to come to another retreat for the rest of her life."

Robin smiled shyly. "At least it's not boring."

Tess smoothly steered the conversation to their upcoming quilt project for a veteran. The women had selected a complex pattern for the quilt, and they planned to start and finish it on Saturday. Even though there were differing opinions about whether or not they could actually get it done in one day, the acrimony of a few minutes earlier had vanished.

Brenda snuck a peek at her cousin. Libby was laughing over something Millie was telling her about the last Houston quilt show.

As always, nothing Brenda had said had affected Libby in the least.

Robin

Friday's book fair was full of people. It was set up in a two-room storefront in downtown Magnolia Harbor, and Robin was amazed at how many books and booksellers were crammed inside. Most of the vendors had only a folding table or two, but fiction and nonfiction books of every genre were stacked on and under the tables and boxes of books were piled behind them. It was glorious chaos, and she wished she had days to search through everything.

Robin passed by a table stacked with books about art and graphic design. She was tempted by a book about writing and illustrating children's stories, but she decided to wait. She could find it and any of the rest of them in the bookstore near her house.

A table of craft books reminded her of the class she'd sat in on yesterday about strip piecing. At first, Robin had been reluctant to attend, but she was glad she had because she'd found it pretty interesting. She was also glad that she'd joined her mother and the other ladies for breakfast and dinner yesterday. She'd had a surprisingly good time sharing two meals with them.

Smiling, she decided to surprise her mom with a book about quilting. As Robin combed through the stacks of books, she noticed one that highlighted quilts in bold colors and patterns. It made her think of Wanda's new quilt design that she'd shown her after class yesterday. Robin had been impressed by the fabrics Wanda had chosen and how well the color combinations worked.

Robin finally settled on a book for her mom. It was about patchwork quilts and featured gorgeous color photographs.

After paying for her purchase, Robin continued to stroll. Soon she spotted another table that interested her. There was something about vintage books that always drew her closer. She didn't recognize many of the titles, though several of them intrigued her. The books that were familiar to her were ones she already owned, and each of them brought back a cherished memory and a desire to visit that story once again.

She was rummaging through the last of the boxes at the table when she found a book that had been one of her favorites when she was Katie's age. It was part of The Chronicles of Narnia, a seven-book fantasy series by C. S. Lewis.

Robin dug through the box until she found all the books but *The Last Battle*, the final volume in the series. It was her favorite, and Jason had always told her that it was the most important. She loved the book so much that she'd even tucked it into her suitcase before coming to the retreat.

The hardcover books were lovely. They were clearly not new, but they were in great shape. Even though she already owned the entire series, she wanted this particular set, including the final volume.

"Excuse me," Robin said to the white-haired man behind the table. "Do you happen to have the last book in this series?"

The man peered over his glasses at the books she had discovered. "It should be in the same box those were in. Did you look through everything in the box?"

"I think so, but maybe I missed it. I searched through it a couple of times."

"Let's take a peek, shall we?" he asked, a twinkle in his eyes. "I have so many books that even I don't know everything about them."

Robin smiled.

The man lowered himself to the floor beside the box in question and picked through the books. "I'm afraid you're right. It's not here.

It really would be a shame to have all the others and not the last one. Now let me think . . ."

She waited patiently, hoping he'd be able to find the book.

The man scanned the other boxes. Suddenly his eyes brightened. "I think this one might be our culprit." He tapped a box that was on the very bottom of a stack against the wall, and then he struggled to his feet.

"Let me," Robin said. She moved the boxes that were on top of the one he had indicated.

The man opened the box and dug around inside it. Finally, he made a little exclamation of success. "There you are," he said, handing her the final volume of the series. "And that makes seven."

"Oh, thank you," Robin said. "Out of all these boxes, how in the world did you know where it would be?"

"These books were packed by my granddaughter, and I remember her telling me that box had some extra room in it. She's a dear girl, but she's never understood the importance of keeping books in logical places. Still, no harm done." He smiled. "Now, what do you think? Would you like to purchase those?"

Robin nodded, and then she winced slightly. "But I don't see a price on them. Usually if you have to ask how much something is, then it means you can't afford it."

"Oh no," the man told her. "I never put prices on my books. When someone is interested enough to ask about a book, I decide what the right price is. You seem to really want them."

"I do, but I already have a set at home so I'd like these for a gift. I believe every child should read them, don't you?"

The man's eyes grew brighter. "Definitely."

"So . . . ?"

"Seven dollars," he said decisively.

She gaped at him. "What?"

"Seven books, seven dollars." He smiled. "That seems about right to me."

"But that doesn't seem fair," Robin protested.

He frowned. "Do you think it's too much?"

"No," she said, laughing. "It's not nearly enough."

"I know what they're worth," he said, patting her arm as she clutched the books to her chest. "And I know it's more than just money. You take them."

"I can't tell you how much I appreciate it," Robin said, overwhelmed with gratitude.

"Don't mention it," the man said. "I hope they'll be enjoyed."

"They will be," Robin said as she paid him in cash.

He put the books in a bag for her and then wrote out an old-fashioned receipt, the kind with the little piece of carbon paper between the original and the merchant's copy. It perfectly suited the purchase.

After thanking him again, she walked down the aisles perusing the other tables. She spotted books that interested her but nothing she was prepared to buy. She had just crossed into the second of the storefront's two rooms when she heard two familiar voices calling her name.

Katie and Will ran to her and hugged her around the legs.

"How come you're here?" Will asked.

"Because I wanted to check out the books," Robin answered.

Katie pointed at the bag Robin was carrying. "What did you get?"

"It's a surprise."

Rick smiled at Robin over their heads. "We didn't expect to see you here."

Robin smiled back at him. "I didn't expect to see you either. Isn't this book fair fun?"

"It is." He held up two bags. "We never seem to get out of these places without buying something."

"We got you a present," Will announced.

"You weren't supposed to tell," Rick said with a grin.

Will clasped his hand over his mouth, eyes big.

Katie giggled.

"Now that you've successfully interrogated Will," Rick said with a teasing look at his son, "you might as well have it." He handed Robin one of the bags.

"You really shouldn't have," Robin said, wondering if his wife knew about this gift.

"No, I should. You've spent a lot of time with the kids, and we all appreciate it." Rick nodded toward the bag. "Go ahead and take a peek."

Robin reached inside the bag and pulled out the book on writing and illustrating children's books. "Oh, thank you!" She leaned down to give both children a hug. "That's so sweet. I looked at this one earlier and almost bought it."

"We're glad you didn't," Will said.

"Yes, we are," Rick said, his eyes warm. "It's not much, but we hope you'll like it."

"It's wonderful," Robin assured him. "I will definitely go through this and see if it makes me brave enough to attempt writing and illustrating a book. At least I'll find out what's involved."

"Now can we see what you got?" Will asked, pointing at Robin's bags.

"You're not supposed to be nosy," Rick told him. He glanced at Robin. "Sorry. You don't have to answer that."

"Actually," Robin said, swinging one of the bags, "I was hoping I could tell you about these." She reached into the bag, removed the most well-known book in the series, and held it out for the children to see.

They peered at the cover.

"*The Lion, the Witch and the Wardrobe* by C. S. Lewis," Rick said. "I used to love The Chronicles of Narnia. I haven't thought about those books in years."

"What's Narnia?" Will asked.

"Oh, it's a magical place where the animals talk and children go on amazing adventures," Robin said.

"There's a lion on the cover," Will remarked. "What's his name?"

"Aslan," Robin said. "He appears in all the books."

"All the books?" Katie asked, trying to peek into the bag.

"All seven of them." Robin handed the bag to Rick.

"You don't mean it," he said. "The whole series? I can't let you do that."

"Of course you can," she said with a grin. "That's why I bought them."

"But they cost—"

"A lot less than the book you just gave me," she assured him. "The man I got them from gave me a great deal. Please take the books. I want the kids to have them."

"They're incredible stories," Rick said. "I don't know why I've never thought of getting them for the kids. Thank you." He faced his children. "What do you say?"

"Thank you, Miss Robin," Katie said.

"Thank you," Will repeated. "Will you read them to us?"

"That would take a long time," Robin said. "But I'm sure your daddy will read them to you."

"I definitely will." Rick smiled at her. "And I'll probably enjoy them as much as the kids, if not more."

"I wouldn't be surprised," Robin said, remembering the author's dedication in the first book. He had said that the girl it was dedicated to was probably too old for fairy tales, but one day she would be old enough to start reading them again.

That sentiment contained hope, a hope Robin had allowed herself to forget. She would have liked to read the books to Katie and Will, to relive the stories through their eyes. It was good to know that Rick loved the books too. They were something families should experience together. But she wasn't part of their family, and she never would be.

She smiled tightly. "Anyway, I thought you'd all enjoy them. And I'm glad I ran into you here, just in case I don't see you before I go home."

"But what about the rest of the books at the fair?" Katie asked, clinging to her hand. "We haven't seen them all yet."

"Well, I should—" Robin said.

"Did you see all the books yet?" Will interrupted.

"Not in this room," she admitted.

"You're more than welcome to join us," Rick said. "I mean, unless you have other plans."

Book fairs were certainly more fun with friends than without. Robin didn't want to leave yet, especially since the week was coming to an end. She might see them around the lake between now and Sunday, but that would be the last of it. Then she'd be going home. They'd be going home. She wouldn't see any of them ever again.

Robin slid the book Rick had given her into the bag with the quilting book for her mom and then took Will's hand. "No, I don't have any plans."

19

Grace

The aroma filling the kitchen was absolute heaven. Grace closed her eyes, trying to identify what was cooking—Italian sausage, bell pepper, onions, basil. She peeked into the oven. Potatoes and tomatoes and cheese too. It was another casserole. Judging from this week's meals, quilters were like church ladies and always had the best practical recipes.

"Doesn't that look delicious?" Charlotte asked, taking a bowl of strawberries from the refrigerator and setting it beside the cutting board. "It doesn't contain many ingredients, and the woman who made it told me she just cuts everything up and tosses it in together and lets it bake. Maybe I need to put some simple recipes like that into my new cookbook."

"I guess that depends on if you're writing for busy people or those who want to spend a lot of time on gourmet creations."

Charlotte started slicing strawberries swiftly and efficiently. "I suppose I don't really do the quick-and-easy thing, do I? Maybe someday I should write a no-fuss gourmet cookbook."

Grace grinned. "You could always try it."

Charlotte blew a strand of hair out of her face. "I'd better save that for later on. First I have to figure out what to do with the book I'm working on. I don't have even half as much content as I need."

"You still have time, right?"

"Yes, but I don't want to wait until the last minute." Finished with the strawberries, Charlotte began cutting up bananas. "Do you remember that sauce Grandma used to make for chicken?"

"I sure do," Winnie said as she entered the kitchen. She hugged her nieces. "What about it?"

"I'm trying to come up with new recipes for my book," Charlotte answered. "Maybe I could do a variation of the sauce with a little sprucing up."

Winnie smiled. "She'd be thrilled to know other people were enjoying it."

"I think so too." Grace picked up the dishes and tableware waiting on the counter. "I'll go ahead and set the table."

"Or you could let one of the ladies do it," Charlotte suggested.

"I could, but it's not a big deal for me to take care of it," Grace said. "I'd hate to interrupt them when they're having such a good time."

"It's been nice having them here." Charlotte's warm smile turned a little bit wry. "Mostly."

"What do you mean?" Winnie asked, raising her eyebrows. "How's the retreat going?"

"Robin seems to be enjoying herself more than I thought she would," Grace said. "But I don't think things are improving between Brenda and Libby."

"I'm afraid not." Charlotte started skewering slices of strawberry and banana on decorative toothpicks and arranging them on a serving platter. "If Brenda came here to patch things up with her cousin, it backfired on her."

"I suppose so," Grace said, disappointed to think that coming to the inn had made their problem worse rather than better. "But they're both still here. I have to believe that means there's still a chance they'll at least talk."

"We can always hope," Winnie said, then glanced around the room. "Is there anything I can do to help?"

"Thanks, but I have the table setting covered." Grace carried the dishes and tableware out to the veranda and started setting the table. When she finished, she heard a hesitant voice at the door.

"Excuse me."

She turned to see Brenda behind her. "Is there something I can do for you?"

"We just realized it was nearly time to eat," Brenda replied. "I was wondering if you were ready for a couple of us to help you and your sister get things ready."

"It's been really nice having all of you help us," Grace said with a smile. "I almost feel like a guest myself."

Brenda gave her a shy smile. "It's not like we've done much."

"But it is a lot of help. Still, I'm through here. Charlotte has everything almost ready in the kitchen. We'll come get you all in a few minutes."

"Thank you," Brenda said, but she remained standing in the doorway.

After a moment, Grace sat down at the table and pulled out the chair next to her. "Would you like to talk?"

Brenda sat down. "I'd like to, but I don't know what to say. It's just—" She put a hand up to her trembling lips. "You've been so gracious listening to my family mess, and I've tried to follow your advice, but I'm afraid it's not working."

Grace reached over and patted her arm. "You know, we all have a family mess of some kind. We all make mistakes. We all say things we wish we hadn't. But only a few of us have the courage to try to work things out, especially with someone who has made it clear she's not interested."

"That's the problem," Brenda said. "Libby isn't interested. She's perfectly happy with things being exactly the way they are between us."

"I haven't been around the two of you when your group has been sewing and having technique demonstrations and everything," Grace said. "How has it been? How has she acted toward you?"

Brenda dropped her gaze. "She either ignores me or makes cutting remarks directed at me."

"Why do you think she says those things?"

"To hurt me," Brenda answered.

"And why do you think she wants to hurt you?" Grace asked gently.

There was no humor in Brenda's laugh. "Because she's still mad at me about the sewing machine and everything else."

"I think Libby is hurting," Grace said gently. "And that's why she wants to hurt you too. But if she didn't still care about you, she wouldn't waste her time on you."

There was a tiny flicker of hope in Brenda's expression. "Do you think so?"

"Don't fool yourself."

Grace turned to see Libby leaning against the doorframe, one hand on her hip, her eyes hard, a cold, malicious smile on her lips.

"Libby," Brenda said with a surprising amount of calmness. "I didn't see you there."

"No, I suppose not," Libby said. "Otherwise, you wouldn't have been talking about me behind my back."

"It wasn't like that. I just . . ." Brenda faltered and looked pleadingly at Grace.

"We were talking about why Brenda came to the retreat in the first place," Grace said, keeping her tone pleasant and conversational.

"Oh, right." Libby gave her a sour smile. "Poor Brenda, she only came here to spread peace and sunshine, and her mean old cousin spoiled everything."

"That's not what I said at all," Brenda protested. "If you'd only let me explain—"

"I'll tell you something, Brenda Clifton," Libby interrupted. "You can do whatever it is you want. I'm done with you. I was the one who took care of Grandma until she died. Me, not you. I guess she'd be really proud to see you airing family business in front of anybody who'll give you the time of day."

"I guess she wouldn't like seeing how things are between us," Brenda said softly.

"She never did see through you," Libby replied. "You and your mother and your whole family."

"What do you mean?" Brenda asked. "We all loved her. We all loved you."

"I know how it was. You threw a crumb or two my way because you felt sorry for me. I didn't have a father or even a mother, so you thought you had to be nice to me." Libby's eyes were ice-cold. "I can do without your charity, thank you very much."

"It wasn't charity," Brenda insisted. "Please, Libby, can't we talk?"

"It looks to me like you've been talking enough for both of us." Libby turned to Grace, her mouth prim. "You seem interested in gossip, so I'm willing to bet that you wouldn't mind hearing some more."

Grace felt uncomfortable, but she kept her expression open and serene. "I've only been trying to help. And if you'd like to talk about anything, I'd be happy to listen."

Libby went to the opposite side of the table and sat down. "I'm sure she already told you my father dumped my mother and my mother dumped me. And when Grandma died, the rest of the family dumped me too."

Brenda gaped at her cousin.

Libby glanced at Brenda. "Deny it if you want to."

"You know that's not true," Brenda said.

"Who took care of Grandma when she was dying?" Libby asked. "It wasn't you. You hardly even came to see her."

"How can you say that?" Brenda said. "You knew that I had my own mother to take care of and I was hardly able to leave the house the last two years she was alive."

Libby waved her hand dismissively.

"Now I don't know if you've convinced yourself that I didn't want to be with you and Grandma or if you just want to be cruel," Brenda continued. "We used to talk over the phone about how hard it was to take care of someone without a break and how much we wished we lived closer so we could see each other more. I knew you were tired. I was tired too."

Libby remained silent.

"I wanted to be there with you when Grandma died," Brenda said, her voice shaking. "But I couldn't leave my mother because there was no one else to take care of her."

"You sure didn't have any trouble sweeping in to pick up your sewing machine once the will was read, did you?" Libby spat.

Brenda pressed her lips together, doubtless not wanting to say anything rash. "Mom was in the hospital by then, and she was being taken care of. I didn't think it would hurt anything to visit you."

"Well, we know how that turned out," Libby muttered.

"Mom asked about you when I got back to the hospital," Brenda said. "I didn't want to tell her what happened. She said she was happy you and I got to spend some time together. She didn't recognize me much after that. I'm glad she never knew about the rift between us."

Libby glared at her.

"One of the last things Mom said to me was that she was so thankful we'd have each other when she was gone," Brenda added wistfully. "She said she didn't want either one of us to be left alone."

Libby stared down at the table, and for the first time Grace thought she looked unsure of herself.

"I tried to tell you all of this before," Brenda said. There was a desperate plea in her eyes. "I tried. Scout's honor."

Her face suddenly hard, Libby shoved back her chair and stood up. "I don't know why it matters anyway. You got what you wanted. You got your sewing machine. I hope you're happy with it." Without another word, she marched out of the room.

Brenda put her head in her hands. "I should never have come here. Nothing will ever change."

"You don't know that for sure," Grace said. "At least she finally heard what you had to say. That's something."

"But is it enough?" Brenda asked.

"I don't know, but it seemed to me like you gave her something to think about." Grace put her hand on Brenda's shoulder and squeezed it lightly. "I know it's not easy, but I believe it's a start."

"I hope so," Brenda said.

Grace stood. "We'd better finish up here before—"

"Your sister walks in and finds out why it's taking so long to set the table." Charlotte stood in the doorway looking comically stern.

Grace laughed.

"The food is ready to be served," Charlotte said.

"I'll round everybody up," Brenda offered, then hurried off.

"Is everything all right?" Charlotte asked, lowering her voice. "Things sounded a little strained in here, and I hated to interrupt."

"There's more tension between Brenda and Libby, I'm afraid. I can see why Brenda is so reluctant to stand up to her." Grace shook her head. "I don't know what to do to help her except listen and pray."

"Those aren't bad options, are they?" Charlotte asked.

"Not bad at all," Grace said, letting out a breath. "As much as I feel for both of them, I'm glad I'm not the one who has to solve their problem."

"I can definitely relate to what Libby's going through," Charlotte said. "It reminds me of how mad I was at Dean when I thought he was stealing my recipes and trying to ruin my reputation. I was carrying a lot of anger and suspicion, and I felt so much better when I realized he wasn't a jerk and we finally worked things out."

"I'm glad you two cleared things up," Grace said as they walked toward the kitchen. "And I'm glad Spencer started out by being our friend."

"Me too," Charlotte said, a twinkle in her eye. "Otherwise, we wouldn't get a supply of fresh pecans."

20

Robin

Saturday morning by Lake Haven was gorgeous. It was glorious September weather. There was a touch of fall crispness in the air. The grass and trees were still clinging to their last greens, and the sun shone brightly on the clear water, making it sparkle and dance with every lapping wave.

"I hate it," Robin said.

Winston blinked at her, clearly hurt.

"Okay, maybe *hate* is too strong of a word," she conceded. "It's a beautiful, peaceful place. An artistic place. A romantic place. I enjoyed spending yesterday at the book fair with Katie and Will, and I know Rick enjoyed it too."

He was a great dad and made sure the kids behaved, but at the same time he wasn't too serious to be silly with them. Or with her. Maybe it had been that talk with Mom that made her see it. He wasn't flirting. He wasn't doing anything but being friendly and fun. But perhaps that was enough.

Robin had made sure she was extra careful too. She didn't do or say anything that could be taken as romantic interest in any way. She still hadn't met his wife, and she couldn't help but wonder why Rick hadn't introduced them. After all, there wasn't much time left. The whole family would be leaving tomorrow.

But none of that had helped.

Once they had left the book fair, Robin had gone back to the inn and up to her room to finish the drawing Rick had asked to buy.

She had spent the whole afternoon finishing it, adding shadows and dimension, details that brought it to life. More than anything, she had wanted to include Rick—the little crinkles at the corners of his eyes when he smiled, the dark curls at the back of his neck, the hint of a dimple that was just like Will's.

At one point, she had started a sketch of Rick—propped up on one elbow as he lay on his beach towel, tanned skin, long legs—but she had scribbled through it and thrown it away before returning to finish the one of the kids. He'd offered to pay her for it, but she had decided by the end of that first day that she'd make a gift of the drawing. She owed him something. He and his children had made the week more than bearable. They'd made it delightful.

"I'll give him the picture," she told Winston. "I'll thank him for his kindness to me, and that will be it. As much as I wish things could be different, it has to be it."

She heard them before she saw them. Katie was singing a song about three little fishies that Robin's grandmother had probably sung as a child. Beside Katie, Will firmly clung to his father's hand. The boy was asking why they had to leave the next day and whether Miss Robin could come with them and if they could read more about Narnia that night before they went to bed.

"Of course," Rick said. "We have lots of books to read now. You two need to make sure to tell Miss Robin thank you."

Seeing her at last, the kids ran over and hugged her.

"Hello, Miss Robin," Will said. "Hello, Winston."

Winston wagged his tail and smiled at them.

The kids giggled and petted the dog.

"Thank you for the books, Miss Robin," Katie said.

"You're very welcome," Robin said. "Are you enjoying them?"

Katie nodded.

"But where's Mr. Tumnus?" Will asked. "They took him away."

"Where could he be?" Robin said. "You'll have to wait and see."

"I'll bet that witch gets Edmund in trouble," Katie said. "She's trying to trick him."

"You'll find out more when we read it tonight," Rick promised. "Right now, why don't you show Miss Robin what you brought?"

Both children were carrying drawing pads and crayons, and they each pulled out a page with a colorful picture on it.

"See?" Will said, thrusting his picture at Robin. "It's a crab doctor."

She admired his interpretation of the drawing she had made for them a couple of days before. The crab doctor didn't have the correct number of legs and his eyes were right in the middle of his shell, but he was definitely holding a needle and thread.

"Wow!" Robin exclaimed. "What a wonderful job you did. It looks almost exactly like the one I showed you. He's ready to sew up his patient."

Will beamed at the praise.

"What is he wearing?" she asked, pointing to what resembled a necklace with a round circle hanging from it.

"That's his heart thing." Will poked himself in the chest. "You know, so he can hear."

"Oh yes, the stethoscope. It's perfect." Robin put her arm around Katie, pulling her a little closer. "And what did you draw?"

"Fishes." Katie grinned as she showed Robin a drawing of several brightly colored fish in blue water with a lot of bubbles.

"Very pretty," Robin said. "And the seaweed is terrific. The fish will have lots of places to play hide-and-seek."

"She needs to put in a shark," Will said. There was more than a hint of mischief in his expression.

His sister scowled at him. "I told you I didn't want a shark. They're bad."

"Not bad," Rick corrected. "Just hungry."

Will laughed.

Katie's frown deepened. "I don't want one."

Rick pressed a kiss to the top of his daughter's head. "You don't have to have one. You get to make your picture any way you want."

"I like both pictures just the way they are," Robin said. "Are you going to hang them up when you get back home?"

"We made them for you." Will thrust his picture at Robin again. "You can hang them up at your house."

"That's a lovely idea," Robin said, accepting the pictures. "Thank you both so much for doing this. It makes me so happy to have pictures that you drew just for me." She gave them each a hug and then put the drawings safely into the back of her sketch pad. "Now, are we going to draw some more today?"

"Yes!" the kids answered in unison.

"Okay, how about some pictures of dogs and cats?" Robin suggested.

When the children agreed, she showed them the examples she had made and told them how she had done them. Then Katie and Will sat under the tree and started drawing their own pictures.

Robin and Rick and Winston sat down next to each other in companionable silence.

"I'm going to hate leaving here," Rick said after a few minutes. "I know the kids are too. They've enjoyed spending time with you."

"I've had fun as well," Robin said, stroking the dog's head. "It's been great while it lasted, but we all have to return to our real lives eventually. It wouldn't be very practical to spend every day simply drawing and relaxing." She looked away, knowing the warmth in his eyes was a reflection of the light in her own.

"Yeah, that's true," Rick said. "And it's time the kids get back to their schoolwork."

Robin frowned. "I hadn't thought of that before. Shouldn't they already be in school for the year? Maybe Will is too young, but Katie's old enough, isn't she?"

"I homeschool both of them," Rick answered. "They have outings and group activities with a group of other kids, but we still have some flexibility on when we take breaks and the kinds of things we study. I'm glad my work schedule allows me to homeschool."

Robin wanted to ask him what he did for a living, but she decided it was probably better not to know. "How are they doing in their schoolwork?" she asked instead.

"Will is just starting, but Katie tested in the top 98 percent for her class recently." He smiled. "So I guess we're doing all right."

"That's great," Robin said. "Oh, I finished your picture of the kids. I hope you like it." She flipped to a different section of her sketch pad and carefully detached the drawing of Katie and Will.

He studied it for a long moment. "That's amazing. It's almost like a photograph. Mama will love seeing this. Now, how much do I owe you for it?"

"It's a gift," she told him, forcing a cheerful tone. She knew this was the end.

"No, really, I want to pay you for it," Rick insisted. "You put a lot of time and effort into it."

Robin shrugged. "I did it because I like your kids, not because I thought I'd make a little money off it. I've never sold any of my work before, and I don't think I could do commercial art anyway. I do it because I like it. Besides, why should I get paid for doing something I enjoy?"

"I think a lot of working artists would disagree with you there." Rick smiled, and his eyes crinkled the way they always did. "But this is a professional job, and I wouldn't feel right if I didn't pay you for it." He cocked his head, the crinkles in his eyes deepening. "Unless we were friends."

She drew back slightly. "I thought we were friends."

"We're acquaintances." He glanced around the idyllic setting. "But it would be nice to be friends in the real world."

Robin had hoped that they could part as casually as they had met. No strings. No regrets. But it seemed he wasn't going to let that happen. She had to address the fact that he was married, but there was no need to be heavy-handed about it. She smiled. "I don't know how your wife would feel about that."

"My wife?"

"Your wife," she repeated, not smiling anymore. Did he think she was an idiot? "You know, the woman you're married to? Your kids' mother? Mama?"

"Mama?" There was more than a little wryness in his soft laugh. "You mean the kids' grandma. My mother."

Robin gaped at him. His mother? "What are you talking about?"

He put one hand on his hip and ran the other through the curls at the back of his neck. "Okay, this is very awkward. I can see why you were confused. I guess we went a little too far by avoiding anything to do with the past."

"So your mother is here with you at The Tidewater?" she asked.

"Yeah. Mama grew up not far from Magnolia Harbor. Most of her friends are out this way, and that's why she wanted to visit. We decided to tag along with her."

"And your wife is where? Back home?"

Rick glanced over at the kids. They were engrossed in their drawings, but he lowered his voice anyway. "She passed away when Will was two."

Her hands tightened on her sketch pad, and her eyes filled with hot, angry tears. "And you didn't tell me?" She pointed at the wedding ring on the third finger of his left hand. "What did you expect me to think?"

"I know, and I'm sorry." He hung his head. "You won't believe me, but I was about to tell you about Cindy and a whole lot of other things the other day. But then Will stepped on a piece of glass and interrupted our conversation. Since then, I've been meaning to bring it up again. I thought maybe we might like to get to know each other better."

Robin stuffed her sketch pad and pencils into her bag. "I think I know everything I need to right now."

"No, you don't," Rick insisted. "Please let me explain."

She glared at him, her breath coming hard, her blood pounding in her ears, but she didn't leave.

"When Cindy died, I wanted to die too, but I couldn't," he said. "I had two little ones to look after and live for. But love? I didn't even want to think about it. I figured if I continued wearing my ring, it would keep Cindy's memory fresh, and it would also be a deterrent to women who were only looking for a good time. If anyone expressed interest in me, all I had to do was show her my ring and say I took it seriously. Then she'd leave me alone, and that was fine by me. I've been doing it so long that I didn't think much about it until recently."

"Why recently?" Robin demanded.

"You said you've had fun with me and the kids. I've had fun too. And I realized how much I've missed having a grown-up to talk to. Besides Mama, I mean."

Her mouth tightened.

"I didn't want to leave here and completely lose touch with you," Rick said. "We don't know each other very well, but I've seen you with the kids. You've been good with them. Not everybody has that kind of patience."

Robin softened the tiniest bit. "They're great kids. I really like them." *And I really like you.*

"I could tell," he said. "It's part of why I was hoping we could keep in touch after we leave the lake. This whole thing about my ring has been a habit. I know it's time to put it away."

"Maybe you should," she said, and then she got to her feet, her bag clutched in two tight fists, "so you don't make a fool out of anyone else."

Winston stood up when she did, looking bewildered.

"Robin, please. I didn't mean to mislead you," Rick said. "You were the one who didn't want any backstories. I still don't know yours. Please try to understand."

Both kids were staring at them now, their eyes round and worried.

"Are you leaving, Miss Robin?" Will asked, standing up with his paper in his hand.

"You didn't look at our pictures yet," Katie added. "Don't you want to see them?"

Robin shot Rick a hard look and then smiled as she walked over to the kids. "Let's see how you did."

Katie showed her the picture.

"Oh, that's very nice," Robin said. "What a pretty kitten. I like her eyes."

Katie stared at her solemnly.

"Let me see your puppy," Robin said, holding the edge of Will's paper so it didn't turn in the wind. "He's so cute."

"Are you mad at us?" Will asked in a small, unsure voice. "Daddy said you were our friend."

"I am," Robin said, then knelt down and hugged the children. "I like you both very much, and I don't want you to forget that. But I have to go back home tomorrow, so I won't be able to see you anymore."

"Not anymore ever?" Will asked.

"I'm sorry, but I'm afraid not," Robin answered.

"Why?" Katie asked, tears pooling in her blue eyes. "Did we make you mad?"

"Oh no." Robin hugged Katie and Will tighter. "It's nothing like that. It's just when you're an adult, sometimes you have to stop playing and get back to work."

Will tilted his head to one side, a perfect imitation of the way his dad had a few minutes earlier. "Can't you go to work and still be our friend?"

Robin glared at Rick over the kids' heads. This was his fault. "I don't think so," she told Will. "I have to go back to my house, and you have to go back to yours."

"But we have a lot of friends who live in different houses from us," Katie said. "They don't mind."

"I'm sorry, but this is the way it has to be this time," Robin said. "I enjoyed spending time with you. I think your pictures are wonderful, and I hope you show them to your grandma. I'm sure she'll love them too."

"Grandma wanted to meet you," Will said. "She told Daddy to invite you to come over."

"You tell her thank you for me." Robin stood up. "And you tell her to take good care of you." She regarded Rick one last time. He was standing there holding the drawing she had made of the kids, a look of pure misery on his face. "Tell her to take care of your daddy too."

"Robin," he said, his voice low and pleading.

"Come on, Winston," she said, and she turned away and walked back to the inn.

Debbie

One more night and then they'd all be going home. It was already midafternoon on Saturday, and the quilt the women were making for a veteran wasn't even halfway done.

Before they had even started the project, Debbie had been certain that the pattern was too intricate for them to finish the whole thing in one day. Even if they finished the blocks and put the quilt top together, it would still have to be quilted and bound.

However, the slow progress hadn't ruined the cheerful mood in the dining room. The women were working away at the quilt, laughing and talking as their sewing machines whirred.

Even Libby seemed to be in a good mood. Maybe it was because she knew she was the best piecer in the group and the most energetic leader. If anyone could motivate the women to work hard enough to finish the quilt today, it was Libby. Or perhaps she was in high spirits because Brenda hadn't made any more attempts to talk to her.

Debbie had been working with the twins cutting out various pattern pieces, but she mismeasured and miscut so many times that Libby told her to quit making a mess out of everything and sew instead.

But Debbie's sewing was even worse, and after two blocks with crooked seams and mismatched points, Wanda had suggested she should be in charge of ironing the finished pieces so they'd be ready to sew. Knowing she had no business handling a hot iron right now, Debbie had complained of a headache and excused herself.

She had already taken a pill earlier. Okay, she had taken more than one. She didn't remember how many. It didn't matter. Debbie couldn't handle being down here with everyone, knowing they were watching her, wondering about her. Perhaps they knew her secret. She couldn't stand worrying about it anymore.

As Debbie headed for the stairs, she happened to glance toward the reception desk. The hatbox was there still, but it was sitting closer to the edge of the desk than it had been when she had slipped her note into it. Maybe . . .

Glancing around to make sure no one saw her, she hurried over to the hatbox. It took only a second to pull the lid off. Yes, there was a note that hadn't been there before. It was written on a piece of soft yellow paper that had wildflowers along the top. She snatched it up and stuffed it into her pocket. Then she jammed the lid back onto the box.

Debbie forced herself not to run up the stairs. On the way, she peeked at the note. *Praying for you* were the only words she had time to read.

She locked the door to the suite behind her and breathed a sigh of relief. Safely alone, she took out her stash of pills so she could get through the rest of the day. After dinner, Debbie could always say that she needed to get to bed early because she still had a headache. Nobody would think anything of it. Nothing more than they already did anyway. Then tomorrow she could go home and not have everyone watching her, whispering about her, knowing she was taking painkillers.

Debbie went into the bathroom and locked that door too. It would be awful if Libby came into the room and saw her in there. It would be awful if anyone came in, if anyone knew.

Praying for you.

Someone knew. Was it Winnie? Did it matter?

She pulled the note out of her pocket and read the gentle, flowing script.

> *Praying for you. You're not alone. None of your friends, your true friends, will abandon you now. Please let them help however they can. So many people love you and care about you. They want you to be safe and well. You don't have to go through this by yourself. It's not weakness to admit you need help. You're not alone.*

Below the words were three telephone numbers to drug addiction hotlines.

Pressing her lips tightly together, Debbie wadded up the paper, threw it into the toilet, and flushed it. She didn't need that kind of help because she wasn't that kind of addict. She could handle it. As soon as she got home, she'd quit.

Debbie was shaky all over. Achy. She hadn't lied when she told the others that she had a headache.

She swallowed one of the pills, then sank down to the cool tiled floor, willing her body to relax. Just a little while and she'd feel better. Just a little while and she'd be able to get up again.

Just a little while . . .

22

Robin

It was a good thing her mother had agreed to leave Robin on her own this week. Mom had gotten the chance to spend time sewing and talking with her friends while having the satisfaction of getting Robin out of the house and the dark place she had been in for the past several months.

Robin had come to Magnolia Harbor expecting to be bored stiff and then return home and crawl back into her comfortable, gloomy rut. But since she had arrived at the inn, she had realized that the melancholy she had wrapped herself in since Jason's death had become more of a habit than a deeply felt emotion. She still loved and missed Jason. Sometimes she physically ached at the loss of him. But that wound, as deep and agonizing as it had been, had started to scar over.

Staying here had given her time for quiet reflection, and she had allowed herself to simply live without any expectations or conditions. Somehow getting away from her everyday life had made Robin see that it was time to try again. It was time to take a real-life risk. And then that real life had slapped her hard across the face and sent her scurrying back to her hiding place to lick her wounds.

Winston followed Robin from the lake and stayed by her side as she crept into the inn. Robin peeked into the door from the veranda, making sure nobody would see her and want to talk. Apart from the whir of sewing machines and the sound of women's voices from the dining room, the place was still.

Wagging his tail, the dog looked up at her and smiled.

Winston was exactly what she needed right now. Robin knelt down and picked him up. She ascended the stairs quickly, almost running into Wanda as she was coming the other way. From her room, no doubt.

"Hi there," Wanda said, holding up a tiny pair of gold embroidery scissors in the shape of a long-legged stork. "Can't do without these."

Robin nodded, not trusting her voice, and tried to move past her.

"We're all collaborating on a quilt we started this morning," Wanda said. "Our lofty goal is to finish today, so we'd appreciate another set of hands. Or if you don't want to quilt, Kathleen brought some wonderful hand-dyed fabrics to show us. Would you like to see them?"

There was understanding and sympathy in Wanda's blue eyes.

"Thank you for the invitation," Robin said. "But I'm really tired. I think Winston and I are going to take a nap."

Wanda put one hand on Robin's arm. "I'm not trying to mind your business for you, but I can tell something has upset you. Would you like to talk about it? I'm a good listener." She smiled. "And I'm even better at keeping my mouth shut."

If she hadn't been holding Winston, Robin would have hugged the older woman. "I appreciate the offer, but there's nothing anyone can do to help."

"I understand. Sometimes a girl needs to be alone to figure out where to head next. But don't let the hurt keep you down. I don't want you looking back when you're my age and being sorry you were too afraid to take a chance. You grab on to those good things when you can because they may not come around again."

"But what if it hurts too much?" Robin asked, her eyes filling with tears.

"Then you try again." Wanda hugged her and Winston both. "I wouldn't have had Lee if I had stopped with Peter. And I wouldn't have Richie now if I'd stopped with Lee. They've all been a wonderful part of who I am. Even though they've each broken my heart in different ways, I thank God for what they've brought into my life."

Robin nodded against her shoulder and then pulled away. "Thank you."

"If you change your mind, please come downstairs," Wanda said. "We'd love to have you."

As soon as Wanda was gone, Robin hurried from the second floor to the third. She shut herself and the dog inside her empty suite, then sat on the bed and held Winston in her arms. There, in the gloom of the unlit room with the dog's comforting presence, she let herself cry.

It was almost dark when Winston's head jerked up at a click of the doorknob. He jumped to the floor and went to the door as it opened.

"Robin?" Mom stepped inside, frowning into the dimness. "Why are you sitting in the dark?"

Robin blotted her eyes with the shredded tissue she was holding. "I guess I fell asleep. It wasn't this dark when I came up here."

Her mother let the dog out, shut the door behind her, and flipped on the light. Then her frown deepened. "Have you been crying?"

"Yes," she replied, and the tears welled up once more.

"What is it?" Mom came over and sat on the bed beside her, holding her close. "Are you okay?"

Robin nodded, knowing she'd be a blubbering mess if she tried to talk.

"Is it that man you've been talking to? Rick?"

Robin nodded again, unable to hold back a sob.

"Did he hurt you?"

"N-no. Nothing like that. Nothing physical."

"Then what is it?" her mom asked. "Did he say something to you?"

"I found out something," Robin answered, "and I don't think I can ever trust him."

Mom started rubbing Robin's back, her voice low and soothing. "Do you want to tell me about it?"

Even though Robin shook her head, the words started flooding out of her. "He's not married."

Mom choked back a startled laugh.

"It's not funny," Robin chided.

"I know. I wasn't laughing at you. But how many women get interested in a man and then are upset to find out later that he *is* married? I don't suppose a lot of them are mad because he isn't." Her mother hugged her a little tighter. "Did he ever actually tell you he was married?"

"No, but he was wearing a wedding ring, and when he talked about the kids, he kept mentioning 'Mama.' Mama this and Mama that."

"Who was he calling mama?"

"He meant *his* mother."

Mom bit her lip, obviously struggling to keep a straight face.

Robin glared at her.

"Well, you did tell him you didn't want to talk about anything in the past, didn't you?" her mom said.

"Yes, but that's not the point."

"You didn't give him much opportunity to tell you anything."

"That particular piece of information was kind of important," Robin protested.

"Did he say anything about why he wears that ring?" Mom asked. "Was he married?"

"His wife died when the kids were little," Robin answered. "He didn't want to deal with women coming on to him, so he decided to keep wearing his wedding ring."

"And did he finally tell you about his wife?"

"No," Robin said, the memory bringing the heat back into her face. "I mean, yes, he did, but it was after I asked about her. Oh, it's so stupid now."

"What exactly did he tell you?"

"He said he and the kids had enjoyed spending time with me and it would be nice to keep in touch. I assumed he was going to proposition me, so I asked him what his wife would think about that. I thought it would be the best way to make him realize I wasn't interested without tearing into him for being a cheater. That was when he told me she was dead." Tears burned in her eyes. "I've never felt so humiliated in my life."

"I'm sorry," her mother said. "I know you're upset with him, but I guess I'm feeling relieved that you aren't getting attached to a married man."

"You don't have to worry about that," Robin told her. "He's too big of a jerk for me to even think about him anymore."

"Now, honey—"

"It's true." Robin shrugged out of her mother's embrace. "He is."

"And what do you base that on?" Mom asked, arching one eyebrow.

"He lied to me!"

"Did he?"

"Okay, he didn't actually lie, but he led me to believe things," Robin said. "That's almost the same as lying."

"I don't know." Mom reached over and took Robin's hand, probably to keep her from pulling away again. "You told me you weren't interested anyway and you were going to make sure he knew it. Why should he even say anything about his wife?"

Robin shrugged, not wanting to be logical.

"Or is it a problem because you were okay with liking him when you thought there was no danger of him liking you?" her mother asked. "When you could get rid of him by mentioning his wife as soon as you felt the least bit of interest in him?"

Tears pooled in Robin's eyes as she looked down.

"Or," Mom said, using one finger to gently tilt Robin's head up, "is it because you've realized that you do like him and the idea of getting involved with someone else scared you?"

"Jason and I would have been on our honeymoon right this minute." Robin rubbed her eyes. "How can I possibly be thinking about some other guy?"

Mom embraced her. "It's all right to move on when the time comes. It's all right to pick yourself up and try again. In fact, it's not just all right. It's something you need to do."

"But I don't know anything about Rick," Robin said. "He could be anyone. He could be an ax murderer."

"You won't discover what he's like until you get to know him and let him get to know you," Mom reminded her.

"I'm not ready for another relationship," Robin said. "And I'm not sure if I'll ever be ready."

Mom pushed a wisp of hair off Robin's forehead. "I'm not saying you should marry the guy tomorrow. But maybe it wouldn't hurt to have dinner with him sometime. Or go with him and the children to the movies. Spend time together doing normal things."

"I don't even know where he lives," Robin said.

"Ask him," her mother said. "He's the first guy you've noticed since Jason died. It's not wrong to find out if you really like him."

"Mom—"

"No, you don't have to tell me what you're going to do," her mom interrupted. "You don't have to decide anything right this minute. I just want you to think about it."

"Okay," Robin murmured.

"Now, are you ready for dinner? I think it's Wanda's chili, and I'm never quite sure what's going to be in it. She changes the recipe every time she makes it."

Robin shook her head. "I'm not hungry. Maybe I'll eat something later."

"All right. But promise me you'll think about what I said." Mom stood up and touched her lips to Robin's forehead. "All I ask is that you be honest with yourself." She walked out the door.

Robin sat for several minutes in the quiet room, not moving, only thinking. Then she got out her suitcase and put it on the bed. She retrieved the copy of C. S. Lewis's *The Last Battle* from inside. This was the final book in the Narnia series, the one that had been missing when she first found the set at the book fair. The best one, the one that gave meaning to everything that had happened earlier in the series.

She opened the book to the photograph that marked her page. It was a picture of Jason hanging upside down from a tree. Robin was standing on her tiptoes in the grass with her face turned up for a kiss. The guy who would have been his best man had snapped the picture just as Robin's lips touched Jason's. The photo was sweet perfection, and she hadn't gone anywhere without it since Jason's death.

"Would you really want me to find someone else?" she whispered, gazing at the photo.

Gotta live.

She heard the words almost as if Jason were still alive and standing next to her. He had said that anytime he was about to try something new, something that in most cases she was afraid to try herself.

Gotta live.

What was Robin going to do about Rick? She had already told him that she didn't want to see him again. It was more than likely that he would take her at her word and leave her alone. But perhaps that would be for the best. Maybe the only reason he had been here this week was to get her to climb out of the rut she'd been in since Jason's death and realize that her life wasn't over yet.

Or maybe it was worth the risk to tell Rick that she was ready to find out if there could be any kind of connection between them. Her mom was right about the possibility scaring her, but it also sent a little spark zinging through her.

After Robin touched her lips to Jason's picture, she put it back between the pages of the book.

Then she decided she was hungry after all and headed downstairs. Even Wanda's mystery chili sounded pretty good.

23

Debbie

Someone was knocking on the door. Debbie thought whoever it was had been knocking for a long time. Whoever it was needed to go away. She wished to be left alone. She was cold and sick and wanted to sleep for days.

"Debbie," Libby called, "are you in there?"

Why didn't she go away? Debbie tried to lift her head from the bathroom floor and tell her she wanted to remain alone in the cold and the dark. Why was it dark? It must already be time for dinner. No wonder Libby was looking for her.

"Go away," she said as clearly as she could. *Go away. Go away. Go away.*

"Debbie!" Libby shouted. "Let me in!" She rattled the doorknob. After a pause, there was a click of metal on metal and more rattling. Then suddenly Libby was kneeling down on the bathroom tiles with one hand on Debbie's forehead and the other pressing her wrist. "What's wrong? What happened?"

Debbie tried to smile. She should always smile. But for some reason, she couldn't right now. "Don't hate me," she mumbled. "Please don't hate me. I couldn't help it."

"What is it?" Libby said, trying to hold Debbie's head up. "Tell me."

Debbie tried to tell her. She needed to tell her, but she couldn't seem to catch her breath.

"Can you hear me?" Libby asked. Her voice sounded strange, and there was something in it that Debbie had never heard before.

Libby slapped Debbie's wrist, but Debbie hardly felt it. Then she was sure there was someone else in the room. It was Brenda. She shouldn't have come. Libby wouldn't like it.

Brenda felt Debbie's forehead and held her wrist for a few seconds. She asked Libby a lot of questions she didn't know the answers to.

"Call 911," Libby directed.

"While I'm calling," Brenda said, "stay with her and make sure she's warm."

Libby gently put a towel under Debbie's head. Then Libby covered Debbie with another one. It was a big, luxurious towel that felt decadent. Just like the towels they used at spas.

"The ambulance is coming," Libby said, taking Debbie's hand. "Brenda's calling them."

Debbie nodded. "I'm glad she's here. You should tell her you're sorry." Her eyes were shut, so she couldn't see Libby's face. Maybe it was better that way.

She could hear Brenda speaking to someone on the phone. She was talking about somebody who was breathing slowly, someone with cold, clammy skin, a weak pulse, and very small pupils. She said that person's breathing wasn't rattling. Debbie guessed that was good.

When Debbie opened her eyes, she was vaguely surprised to see Libby watching over her. There was worry in her expression. Libby never worried. Libby was never anything but perfectly sure of herself. Maybe she was worried about whoever Brenda was talking about on the phone. Still . . .

"You ought to tell her you're sorry." Debbie squeezed Libby's hand. "She didn't take your pills. I told you that already."

"That doesn't matter right now," Libby said. "You need to lie still and relax. We can talk about it later." She glanced up at something. Brenda maybe. Brenda was still talking.

"She didn't take your pills," Debbie repeated. "I took them. And Tess's. And other people's too. Whatever I could get."

"Please rest," Libby insisted. "We'll discuss it later when you're feeling better."

Brenda was standing next to her and Libby. Debbie could see her shoes, a pair of practical slip-ons that didn't need to be tied. For some reason, Brenda wasn't talking anymore.

"You should tell her you're sorry," Debbie murmured.

Libby didn't say anything.

Brenda asked her something, and Libby finally answered her. But Debbie couldn't hear what they said because their voices were too low.

After a moment, Brenda said, "Yes, still here. About the same, a little more alert . . . really drowsy."

Was she talking on the phone again? Debbie couldn't tell, but she hoped they would both go away and leave her alone. Neither of them was listening to what she said anyway.

Debbie felt someone touch her sleeve, and she opened her eyes.

"There's an ambulance coming," Brenda said, kneeling down beside her. "Can you hear me?"

Debbie nodded. She heard, even if Brenda seemed a long way away.

Then there was a lot of noise. A lot of people. Loud people who kept asking her questions and pulling her around, poking her with needles and wrapping her in blankets.

"Anyone coming to the hospital with her?" one of them asked.

To Debbie's surprise, Libby said she was.

"Do you want me to come with you?" Brenda asked.

Libby answered, but Debbie couldn't hear the words.

"I'll be here when you get back," Brenda promised.

Libby didn't answer her at all that time.

One of the people told Libby they'd take care of everything, but Libby still didn't answer.

After that, Debbie was in the ambulance. There were so many lights and noises.

It was a long time later when Debbie realized Libby was beside her once more. Debbie knew they were in the hospital because of the bright lights and the constant sound of hurrying footsteps.

"They're going to put you in a room now," Libby told her. "They're going to make sure you're all right."

Debbie wasn't sure if she felt better or worse. She wanted to sleep. But how could she sleep yet? "I have to tell you about Brenda. She didn't take your pills."

"I know," Libby said, her voice uncharacteristically subdued. "Debbie, why didn't you tell me about this? I didn't even realize you were having a problem. I didn't see it."

Debbie could manage only a faint smile. She had to smile, no matter what. "Doesn't matter."

"It does matter." Libby's voice was low and fierce. "I could have done something to help you."

Debbie shook her head. It was such a tiny gesture that she wondered if Libby would even notice. "Weak," she breathed. "Liar. Thief. Didn't want you to hate me."

Then she realized Libby's hand was clasping hers. No, not one hand but both hands were clinging to Debbie's.

"I didn't mean that," Libby said. "I didn't mean that about you. I didn't know it was you."

"Don't hurt Brenda anymore," Debbie said. "Don't cut yourself off from everybody who cares about you. Everybody who loves you. Or who wants to, if you'll let them."

She heard the slither of the rings on the curtain that gave the room a little bit of privacy.

"Ms. Milner?" It was a man's voice, loud and unrelentingly cheerful. "We're going to put you in a room now. You'd better say good night to your friend. We'll make sure to let her know when you can have visitors."

"I'll be back," Libby said, trying to pull her hand away.

But Debbie held on to it for a moment longer. "I don't want you to wind up alone," she whispered, and then she felt the slight vibration of the bed as it rolled into the corridor.

Behind her, she heard Libby start to cry.

24

Robin

The final thing Robin packed in her suitcase Sunday morning was her copy of *The Last Battle*. After dinner the night before, she had returned to her room and read it from beginning to end.

She had lost track of how many times she had already read it, before Jason's death and after, but there was always something new that struck her with every reading. This time it was when she read about Jill Pole realizing she wasn't going to survive the coming war and deciding it was better to die for what she loved than "grow old and stupid at home . . . and then die in the end just the same."

That was so much like Jason. *Gotta live*. He wouldn't have been afraid to tell someone how he felt. He had never let fear hold him back.

Still, did Robin dare go over to The Tidewater and talk to Rick? What if he and his family were already gone? The more time she let slip away, the more likely it was that they had left for home. She had no idea where they lived. Rick Collins. The name was all she knew. How many Rick Collinses were there in the area? In the state? In the whole country? If she didn't find him and talk to him soon, she'd most likely never see him and the kids again.

She went to the bathroom door. "Mom?"

"I'm almost ready."

"I was wondering if you're in a hurry to leave."

Mom opened the bathroom door. "No, I was hoping to stay until Libby returns from the hospital. I want to hear how Debbie is doing." She cocked her head. "Why do you ask? Is there something you wanted to do?"

"Don't make a big deal out of this," Robin said. "But I thought I'd go over to The Tidewater and see if Rick's still there. If nothing else, I owe him an apology."

Mom didn't gush or ask any questions. She merely nodded. "Take your time. We'll leave whenever you're ready."

"Thank you," Robin said, grateful for her mother's subdued reaction. She rushed out of the room. As she descended the second flight of stairs, she met Grace.

"I was just coming upstairs to find you," Grace said. "There's someone here to see you. He's wondering if you'll talk to him for a few minutes."

"Really?" Robin asked, stunned.

Grace nodded. There was a touch of a smile on her lips. "He's waiting outside by the lake."

Robin flew down the stairs, then sped out the back door and out to the lake.

Rick was leaning against the big magnolia tree. When he saw her on the veranda, he appeared a bit surprised. "Hi," he said, pushing himself away from the tree and coming toward her. "I didn't know if you'd talk to me or not."

"I wasn't sure if you had left yet." Robin felt more than a little uncomfortable. "Where are the kids? Are they with your mother?"

"Yes, she's helping them pack before we go home," he explained. "I told her I'd be back in a few minutes. You and your mom must be about to head out too, so I won't keep you long."

"It's all right," she told him. "Mom wants to stay longer because one of her friends was rushed to the hospital last night."

There was instant concern in his expression. "I'm sorry. Is her friend all right?"

"I'm not sure," Robin answered. "One of the other ladies went to check on her. I don't know when she'll be discharged."

There was an awkward silence between them.

Finally, Rick cleared his throat. "I wanted to tell you I'm sorry. I didn't mean to be deceptive with you. Honestly, I left the ring on when I met you because I wasn't interested in anything but the drawing you did of the kids. When they had so much fun with you, I didn't think it would hurt anything if we talked. But knowing we weren't going to see you anymore by the end of the week, I realized that was something I didn't want to happen. I was going to tell you about Cindy, but I didn't get a chance before everything blew up in my face."

Robin remained silent as she studied Rick, giving him a chance to go on.

"Anyway, I appreciate the time you've spent with the kids," Rick said. "With Mama visiting her own friends during our stay, I've been scrambling to keep them entertained. And getting to like you so much in the meantime was an especially nice bonus." He bit his lip. "I wish we'd had time to become friends. That's all. I feel like I've messed up a chance for something that might have been really nice."

Robin regarded him for another long moment. She was afraid to say anything, yet she was afraid not to. Then she turned and walked to the veranda. She sat down and patted the chair next to her.

Rick followed and took the seat beside her.

"Will you tell me about your wife?" she asked.

His expression was bittersweet. "We got married right out of college and had Katie a couple of years later, then Will. It was kind of hard to manage on just my paycheck, but we both wanted her to be able to stay home with the kids. She had majored in education, so it was important to her to teach the kids herself. She never got a chance, because they were still pretty young when she died."

"What happened to her?" she asked.

"Cancer. It's not something you'd expect with somebody as young and healthy as she was, but it can hit anybody."

"My dad had cancer," Robin said softly.

"Yeah, so did mine."

"I'm sorry."

"Thank you," Rick said. "I'm sorry for your loss too."

They were quiet for a few moments.

"When Cindy passed, my mother moved in with me and the kids," he said. "It's worked out pretty well for both of us. To be honest, I don't know what I'd do without her help, and the kids love her."

"I'm sure they do," she said. "You've both done a great job with them."

"Thanks."

Robin took a deep breath. It was time to let Rick know about her past. "I want to tell you about my fiancé, Jason. If he were still here, we would be on our honeymoon right now."

"I'm really sorry."

"Thank you," she said.

"How did you two meet?" Rick asked.

"Jason and I went to school together all the way through college. Our families had gone to the same church for years. Mom even liked him, and that wasn't something you could say about every guy I went out with. I think she was looking forward to having him as a son-in-law. I don't know how many times he helped her around the house with something she couldn't handle by herself. She always said it was like having a son of her own."

Rick smiled.

Her return smile was shaky. "Not that Jason didn't have his faults, of course. He didn't always think things through, and that got him into trouble more than once. But it was never anything serious, never anything that he didn't take responsibility for and make right. And I know he loved me. I could see it in his eyes every time I was with him."

"What happened to him?"

Robin pressed her trembling lips together. "We had some heavy rains and flash flooding. You've seen those signs that say not to drive into water over the road, haven't you?"

He nodded.

"So many people don't pay attention to the warnings," she said, twisting her fingers together in her lap. "It was so stupid."

Rick was silent as he waited for her to go on.

"Anyway, Jason was driving home in his truck. It was pouring rain. The kind of rain that comes down in sheets, making it really hard to see. The car in front of him got washed off the road and ended up against some trees. He tied a rope to the back of his truck and went down there to help. A woman and her young son were trapped inside the car. Jason tied the rope to their car, then helped them get to the truck."

"So they were safe," he said.

"They were all safe," Robin clarified. "But Jason said he was going down to untie his rope. The woman begged him not to go. She told him she couldn't believe how strong the current was and that it had swept her car away before she knew what was happening. Jason said he'd be careful, but it wasn't that bad and the rope was still tied to his truck. But then . . ." She shook her head.

"He was gone," Rick finished for her.

"The woman glanced at her son to make sure he was all right, and when she looked up, Jason wasn't there." Tears burned her eyes, and Robin wiped them away. "The police think he must have slipped and lost his grip on the rope." She paused. "It took almost two days for them to find his body."

Robin was surprised to find that telling Rick what had happened to Jason wasn't as bad as she had feared. Actually, it felt good to talk to someone. She hadn't really spoken to anyone but her mother about it. Robin didn't tell Rick everything because she hoped there would be time for that later. But she did share with him her fears and her hopes and how much different she felt now compared to when she had arrived at Magnolia Harbor.

"I don't know what might happen," Robin concluded. "But you've made me see that I'm ready to take a chance again."

Rick smiled as he caught her hand. "Maybe we both just needed to meet the right person."

"So," she said, feeling a touch of warmth in her cheeks, "where do we go from here?"

"Maybe we can let the kids know we're going to stay in touch." He stood and gently pulled her to her feet. "Then perhaps you'd like to meet Mama."

Robin gave him a rueful grin. "I wish I'd met her sooner."

"I'm sorry about that," Rick said, wincing slightly. "Anyway, I know she wants to meet you."

"I'd like that," she said. "And I'm sure my mom wants to meet you and the kids."

"Does that mean we can still be friends after we go home?" he asked.

"I don't know." Robin tilted her head. "Where do you live? I'm from Sangaree."

"We're about twenty minutes away in Knightsville."

She smiled. "That sounds close enough to be friends."

25

Brenda

"Debbie's going to be in the hospital for a while," Libby announced to the quilters when they were gathered in the dining room.

Brenda had never seen her cousin appear so shaken. Finding Debbie in such a serious state had definitely taken a toll on Libby.

"She told me to tell all of you she'd love to see you sometime but not right now," Libby continued. "She, uh, has some things she needs to work through first."

"But she's going to be okay, isn't she?" Tess asked.

Libby nodded. "She wanted me to apologize to you in particular. For taking your pills."

"I wish I had known she was having such a hard time," Tess said. "I would have tried to help her."

"We all would have," Carolyn said. "I hate going back home and just leaving her here."

"None of us lives too far away to come visit." Wanda looked purposefully at the others. "But only when she's ready." A gleam came into her eyes. "That doesn't mean we can't make some things to send her to let her know we're thinking of her. We're all pretty handy with our sewing machines."

"Or we could send her books and flowers or something like that," Ellen suggested.

The ladies started discussing what else they might do to make Debbie feel better.

As the women talked, Libby approached Brenda. She stared at

the floor for a moment, then lifted her chin and put on a tight smile. "Would you talk to me for a minute?"

"Of course," Brenda said. She was pleased by her cousin's unexpected request, but she didn't want to get her hopes up.

As they walked out into the lobby, Brenda asked, "Would you like to talk here, or would you rather go upstairs to your room?"

"Perhaps we could sit on the veranda for a minute," Libby replied.

Brenda smiled. "That sounds lovely."

There was a breeze off the lake, and it made the veranda deliciously cool and pleasant.

The two of them sat next to each other for several minutes without saying anything. Brenda didn't dare begin the conversation.

Finally, Libby drew a deep breath and let it out. "All I wanted to say is that I'm sorry."

Brenda was so surprised that she didn't know how to respond. She prayed that her expression was calm and receptive. It wouldn't do for Libby to realize that her heart was thudding like a jackhammer.

"I don't have any excuses," Libby added. "You know I love that sewing machine, but I guess you also know that none of this was ever about that."

"Yes," Brenda said softly.

"I've tended to push you around because I figured you'd always be there no matter what I did." Libby rubbed her eyes. "I recognize I wasn't being very reasonable when Grandma died. She was gone, and then you left me too."

"Oh no." Brenda put one hand on Libby's arm. "No, I never left you. I never wanted things between us to change. I tried to stay in touch, but I felt like you didn't want me to. I tried."

"I know." Libby closed her eyes, and a tear slipped down her cheek. "Grandma passed away, and you were gone. And then your mother died, and I didn't have anybody apart from a few friends. Debbie has been trying to get me to patch things up with you for over a year now, but it wasn't until I found her on the bathroom floor that I realized she could be gone in the blink of an eye too."

"What happened last night?" Brenda said. "You never told me."

Libby removed a tissue from her pocket and dabbed her eyes. "I went to my room to get a sweater and to see if Debbie was coming to dinner. I knew she wasn't feeling very well, but she claimed it was a headache, so I didn't pay much attention."

"I heard her complaining about a headache too," Brenda said.

"The suite was locked, and when I got inside the room, I noticed the bathroom door was locked too," Libby went on. "I could hear her inside the bathroom. It was like she was trying to say something, but the words wouldn't come out right. She didn't unlock the door, so I finally had to use the screwdriver her friend Winnie gave me to take off the doorknob and get inside. I was sure Debbie was going to die."

"She certainly could have if she was as bad as she seemed," Brenda said.

"I was rooming with her," Libby said. "If I hadn't been so concerned with being nasty to you, then I might have noticed how much she needed help."

"Don't blame yourself," Brenda said as she stroked Libby's arm. "You saved her life last night. She might not have made it if you hadn't found her when you did."

Libby glanced away. "Debbie kept telling me that I ought to apologize to you. And she told me she didn't want me to end up alone." She covered her face with her hands.

Brenda wrapped her arms around her cousin. "It's all right," she soothed. "Debbie is getting the help she needs. And I'm still here. I still want us to be friends. I've always wanted us to be friends. Best friends. The way we used to be."

Libby finally looked her in the eye.

"But I didn't want to have to buy your friendship," Brenda continued. "Especially with a sewing machine that should have brought us closer, reminding us of all the fun we'd had with it at Grandma's."

"You're right," Libby said. "And Grandma was right to give it to you. I'm glad you have it."

Brenda cupped Libby's face in both hands. "I want you to have it now. It's in the trunk of Tess's car. I meant to give it to you as soon as I saw you here, but then . . ." She shrugged apologetically.

"Then I had to start acting the way I did." Libby clasped the hand on her cheek. "Oh, Bren."

"It's not a bribe in exchange for you being my friend again," Brenda said. "I want you to have it. Whether or not you think we can work things out otherwise, I want you to have it."

Libby shook her head. "You keep it. It's what Grandma wanted. She'd be devastated if she knew we hadn't talked in so long."

"She definitely would be," Brenda agreed.

"It was difficult when Grandma passed," Libby said, blotting her eyes again. "She had always been there for me. Even when my mother didn't want me, she did. And when she was gone, I felt like everything was upside down. And then I lost you too."

"You never lost me," Brenda said. "I was angry and hurt, but I've missed you so much all this time. I had to try again to let you know how I feel."

"I've missed you too," Libby admitted. "I've wanted to call you, but I—" She grimaced. "After everything I've said to you, I was afraid that you were done putting up with me. I was too proud to tell you how wrong I've been and how foolish all this sounds now."

Brenda hugged her close. "It's only foolish if we let it continue to keep us apart."

For a moment, Libby was still and stiff. Then she relaxed against her cousin's shoulder. "I'm sorry," she whispered. "I'm so, so sorry."

"I'm sorry too," Brenda said, tears spilling down her cheeks. "I'm sorry I didn't hunt you down and make you understand that I love you and I'll stand by you no matter what happens." She smiled through her tears. "Scout's honor."

There was a laugh in Libby's sob. "Scout's honor."

26

Grace

There was quite a commotion that afternoon. Grace wasn't used to every guest in the inn checking out at the same time, but she and Charlotte somehow managed to keep everything moving smoothly.

Finally, there were only five guests left. Brenda and Libby were talking in the Dogwood Suite. Tess and Carolyn were in the reception area waiting for Brenda and Robin.

"I can't very well leave Brenda here," Tess said cheerfully. "All her luggage is in my car, and she doesn't have a ride home."

"I'm sure they'll be done soon," Grace said, then turned to Carolyn. "And I imagine Robin will return soon too."

"I'm not in a hurry," Carolyn said. "I've been waiting for something like this to happen for a while now, and I'm enjoying every minute of it."

She had been smiling ever since her daughter had told her that she was going to meet Rick's mother.

"You're both welcome to stay for as long as you like," Grace assured them. "Charlotte and I love to see our guests leave happy."

"I know I'm certainly leaving that way." Carolyn glanced around the foyer, eyes shining. "I wouldn't dare say this in front of my daughter, but I think it's a miracle. I know it might not end up being anything more than friendship with her and Rick, but it's been wonderful to see her enjoying herself and caring about someone else. I was afraid she'd never start to truly live again."

"It's amazing what a little prayer and common sense will do, isn't it?" Charlotte said. "Sometimes just getting people to think about what they're doing and what they really want is enough to change everything."

Tess shook her head. "I didn't think anything could make Libby get over herself, and now she's actually talking to Brenda. If you ask me, that's a miracle too."

The front door opened, and Robin strolled inside with the kids Grace had seen playing out by the lake recently. With them was the man who had asked Grace to tell Robin he'd like to talk to her. He appeared happy now. All of them did.

"Mom, this is Rick Collins," Robin said. "And, Rick, this is my mom."

Carolyn smiled. "I'm so glad to meet you."

"Same here," Rick said.

"And who are these adorable children?" Carolyn asked as she leaned down to the boy and girl, who clung to their dad and peered at her shyly.

"My kids, Katie and Will," Rick said. "Say hello to Mrs. McAllister."

"Hello," Katie said. "Are you Miss Robin's mommy?"

"I am, and I'm happy to meet you," Carolyn said. "Robin has told me what wonderful artists you both are."

"I drew a robot," Will said, his shyness evidently forgotten. "I can draw you one if you want."

"I'd like that very much," Carolyn answered.

"Is Miss Robin going to come home with us?" Will asked.

Grace bit her lip, trying not to laugh at Carolyn's startled expression.

Rick gave the boy a look.

Robin laughed. "Rick invited me to drive back with them, so we could talk."

"You're not going out of your way, are you?" Carolyn asked, turning to Rick.

He shook his head. "We live in Knightsville, so it's not far."

"You don't mind, do you, Mom?" Robin asked.

"Not at all. Your luggage is already in my car. I'll take it home, and Rick can drop you off when you get there." Carolyn gave them a mischievous smile. "Or maybe Rick's mother and the kids could ride with me, and you two could go together."

"I wouldn't want to do that to you, Mrs. McAllister," Rick said. "I mean, Mama gets along with everybody, but I wouldn't want to make your trip the slightest bit uncomfortable."

"I understand she's a quilter," Carolyn said, "so we'll definitely have a lot to talk about. I'd love to meet her."

"You'll like her," Robin told her mother. "She's very down-to-earth. Sort of the perfect grandma type, you know?"

Carolyn chuckled. "That doesn't tell me a lot, but I'll bet she and I will get along great."

"She's been asking about Miss Robin all week," Katie said.

Will nodded. "She told Daddy it was about time she got to meet her."

Rick gave them an exaggerated scowl.

Both kids giggled.

"I don't know if I dare leave you alone with Mama and the kids," Rick said to Carolyn. "They'll tell you so much about me that I won't have one secret or a shred of dignity left by the time we get home."

"That's okay," Carolyn replied. "I can always keep them busy during the ride by telling them stories about Robin."

"Mom!" Robin protested.

"I think we'll get along fine," Carolyn said with a smile. "What do you think, Katie and Will? Would you and your grandma like to ride back with me?"

"Can we, Daddy?" Will asked. "We'll behave."

"All right," Rick said, giving him and Katie a hug. "But you mind Grandma and Mrs. McAllister, and remember your manners."

"Will you really tell us about Miss Robin?" Katie asked Carolyn, her eyes round.

"I'll tell you about when she was a little girl and had a bird that talked. Now, why don't you two introduce me to your grandma?" Carolyn took both children by the hand and gave her daughter a serene smile. "I'll see you two at home."

"Okay, thanks," Robin said. "Oh, is Wanda still here?"

"She left a few minutes ago," Carolyn said. "Why?"

"I wanted to tell her thank you," Robin answered. "Will you tell her the next time you see her?"

"I'd be happy to," Carolyn said. "Or maybe you could start quilting with me, and then you'd see her all the time. How would that be?"

Robin laughed softly. "You never give up, do you? Well, we'll see about that. For now, would you give her my thanks? And tell her that I want to be just like her when I grow up."

"I'll do that." Carolyn gave her daughter a quick hug. "I was thinking of making spaghetti for dinner, if anyone's interested in staying once we get to our house."

"Spaghetti," Rick said when the three of them were gone. "I think your mom made two new best friends. No, scratch that. Three new best friends, once she says that to Mama."

"Are you sure your mom won't mind riding with her?" Robin asked.

"Positive, but we'd better go out and make sure we've got everybody on the same page." Rick nodded at Grace. "Thank you."

Just then, Winston appeared and made a beeline for Robin. He plopped down at her feet.

Robin knelt down to pet him and then gave him a big hug. "You sure know how to make a girl feel better, Winston."

He snuggled against her and smiled, clearly glad to have been of help.

"Thanks for lending him to me," she told Grace when she stood.

"Anytime. Winston is the most important member of our staff," Grace said. "The inn wouldn't be the same without him."

Winston barked in agreement.

"I think Winston's going to miss you," Charlotte said. "And the kids."

"I'll sure miss him." Robin's smile was a little bit shy. "This is a beautiful place. A good place to think. I hope I'll be able to come back sometime soon."

"You're always welcome," Grace said. "You too, Rick, and the kids."

"I'll keep that in mind," he said, and then he turned to Robin. "Are you ready?"

She hesitated, looking at him searchingly, and then she smiled and took his hand. "Ready."

Rick smiled in return as he ushered her out the door.

"I wish them the best," Tess said softly after they'd left. "After the tragedy Robin's been through, this is definitely a step in the right direction."

"For Robin and Rick both, I hope," Grace said.

Tess motioned toward the stairs. "I guess the longer Brenda and Libby talk, the better."

"They can take their time," Charlotte said. "We don't have the Dogwood Suite booked until tomorrow, and everybody's already checked out from your group, so they're good to go whenever they're done."

"We're done," Brenda said as she and Libby came up to the reception area.

The two of them were both a little flushed, but the look wasn't unbecoming to either of them.

Libby, acting slightly flustered, took Winnie's screwdriver out of her bag and handed it to Grace. "Your aunt was kind enough to loan this to me. She said I could give it to you to return to her. Please tell her thank you for me. I don't know what I would have done without it."

"Winnie's visiting your friend Debbie in the hospital today," Charlotte put in. "She'll be pleased to know the screwdriver came in handy."

"We hope you and your friends will come and stay with us again," Grace said. "This was the first quilters' retreat we've had here, but I hope it won't be the last."

"I'm sure it won't be," Tess said, fishing her keys out of her purse. "Everything was terrific, and the room you set up for us was wonderful." She turned to her companions. "Don't you think?"

Libby nodded. "Lots of room, lots of light, lots of extension cords. It was great." She smiled at her cousin. "Better than I ever expected."

"Me too," Brenda said as she returned Libby's smile.

"I'm so glad things worked out for you," Grace told Brenda and Libby.

"Thank you," Brenda said. "Things worked out so well that I think I'm going to attend the group meetings whenever I can."

"That sounds nice," Grace said. "My aunt enjoys her quilting group, and it makes me think I should go to their meetings more often too." Sometimes she went to The Busy Bees meetings, but she wasn't a regular member.

Charlotte raised her eyebrows.

"But I don't know when I'd ever find the time for it," Grace admitted. "Maybe someday."

"You've got some good teachers in your aunt's group," Libby enthused. "If people would listen to them, then they might learn a lot."

Out of Libby's sight, Tess rolled her eyes.

Grace hid a smile. From what she'd been told, Libby had resisted learning anything from The Busy Bees. Well, nobody could expect Libby to change completely, at least not right away, but perhaps she was a little more open to it now. It was a start.

"One more thing before we go," Brenda said to Tess. "Can I borrow your car keys? I need to get something out of your trunk."

"Be careful when you open it," Tess cautioned as she handed Brenda the keys. "Things are packed pretty tight in there."

"I will."

"I guess I should be heading home," Libby said, taking out her own keys.

"Wait a minute," Brenda said. "Please." She hurried outside and soon came back with a quilt bundled in her arms. "I wanted to show you this." She unfolded the quilt and held it up.

Tess regarded it with a knowing grin.

Libby gaped at the quilt, grabbing one corner of it as if she wasn't sure whether it was real. "How did you do that? You hadn't even finished piecing it yesterday, and now it's quilted and bound and all finished. It's just like the one Grandma made when we were girls."

"I still have to finish the one I've been working on this week," Brenda said. "I had already made this one." She held the quilt out to her cousin. "For you."

For a moment, Libby didn't move. Then she cleared her throat. "For me? Before—"

"Yes, before I knew whether or not you'd talk to me," Brenda said. "Because I hoped." She held out the quilt again.

Libby took it and ran her fingers over it. "Thank you. I think Grandma would be proud of this." Her voice quavered, but she went on. "It's every bit as good as the one she made."

"There's something else in Tess's trunk," Brenda told her. "The sewing machine. I want you to take it to your house. To Grandma's."

"But that's yours," Libby said.

Brenda nodded.

"But—"

"That way you can use it whenever you want, and maybe, if you ask me to come visit sometimes, we can sew on it together. Like we used to."

"But Grandma left it to you," Libby protested.

"I want to respect her wishes," Brenda said, "but that doesn't mean we both can't enjoy it. And I believe it belongs at her house anyway. I think she'd like that, don't you?"

After a moment, a touch of a smile crept across Libby's face. "I know she would, and I'd like it too. You'll have to come over often."

"I'd love to," Brenda said.

Tess looked at them both thoughtfully. "Robin is riding back home with that young man she's been talking to this week. Carolyn and his mother are driving back with his kids to give them a chance to spend some time together. I'm thinking that might not be a bad idea for you two. No need to unpack anything. Brenda, you can ride with Libby, and I'll follow you to her house. Then we can drop off the sewing machine, and after that I'll take you to your house. Fair enough?"

Brenda smiled. "Thank you. It sounds perfect. All right, Libby?"

"That would be good," Libby said. "And if you still like my coffee, then maybe you'd both better come in for a little while when we get to my place."

"I'll definitely take you up on that offer," Tess said. Then she addressed Grace and Charlotte. "The coffee here is delicious, but sometime you ought to ask Libby how she makes hers. It's amazing."

"It's nothing special," Libby said, though the sparkle in her eye belied her humble tone. "But you call me sometime, ladies." She jotted down her phone number on the notepad sitting on the reception desk. "I'd be proud to tell you exactly how I do it."

"It won't do you any good," Brenda chimed in. "I know exactly what she does, and I can never get my coffee to taste as good as hers."

"There's nothing to it," Libby said dismissively, but she was clearly delighted with the compliment.

"You're just like Grandma with coffee," Brenda remarked. "She always said the same thing."

"Well, you and Tess come on over, and we'll see if I've lost my touch or not." Libby gave Grace and Charlotte an almost regal nod. "Tell your aunt what I said about that screwdriver. I don't know how she knew I'd need it."

"It's what she does," Grace said with a smile.

"And we're glad she does," Charlotte added. "We'll tell her you said thank you."

"And tell her we'll be back to see Debbie before long," Libby said.

Grace and Charlotte walked the three women out to the parking lot and saw them off. Then the two sisters went back into the inn.

"So much for our first quilters' retreat," Charlotte said as they walked over to the dining room. "Now to put everything back the way it was."

"It's not so bad," Grace told her. "Just fold up the tables, put away all the power strips, and move the dining table."

"And everything else we moved out of the way."

Grace laughed. "All in all, I think it was a success."

"Definitely."

The two sisters started unplugging and winding up the extension cords.

"Sometimes I wish I knew more about what happens to our guests after they leave," Charlotte mused. "We often witness guests finding fresh starts during their stay, but we don't know what happens to them when they get home."

"Well, you know what Winnie always says about what she does. She's only supposed to give something to someone. What happens after that is none of her business."

Charlotte picked up a tangle of yellow thread that had fallen under one of the chairs. "I'd still like to know."

"Winnie is friends with Debbie," Grace reminded her as she pulled a chair up to the other side of the table. "And Debbie is friends with Brenda and Libby. So maybe we'll hear something about them."

"But what about Robin and the guy she met?" Charlotte asked.

Grace replaced the LED task light on the sideboard with an antique one. "Don't forget that Debbie is friends with Carolyn. So maybe we'll hear something about Robin someday too."

"Or maybe Robin will come back to the inn herself someday," Charlotte suggested. There was a twinkle in her eyes as she set a vase of fresh flowers on the sideboard. "On her honeymoon."

Predicting a wedding for Robin and Rick might seem too soon, but Grace knew it was certainly possible. After all, the Magnolia Harbor Inn regularly worked its magic in the lives of its guests.